The Comp

Puccini

The Complete Puccini

THE STORY OF THE WORLD'S MOST POPULAR OPERATIC COMPOSER

Colin Kendell

AMBERLEY

First published 2012

Amberley Publishing
The Hill, Stroud
Gloucestershire, GL5 4EP

www.amberleybooks.com

British Library Cataloguing in Publication Data.
A catalogue record for this book is available from the British Library.

ISBN 978 1 4456 0445 9

Typeset in 10pt on 12pt Sabon.
Typesetting and Origination by Amberley Publishing.
Printed in the UK.

Contents

Introduction

I've tried to tell the life of Puccini by using his operas as milestones. For each one there is usually a story involved – how he decided upon it and how it was composed. The stories of the operas are outlined and some of the musical content of each one is described. Some of Puccini's arias and duets are among the most popular in the whole of opera and it increases our enjoyment of them when we see how they fit into the stories.

It's possible to see something of the character of Puccini as it was affected by his fortunes as a composer – confident at first when he emerged as a promising young talent, cautious and uncertain after the failure of his second opera had endangered his career, gradually more assured as he became established as a leading musical figure, then, at the end, anxious to complete his final work as if he sensed that illness might put an end to his life before he could do so.

Puccini was a contradictory character – apparently cavalier in his approach to life, with his many affairs with women, but also subject to feelings of great depression. The depressive side of his nature, however, usually showed itself in connection with his work, when a project seemed to have reached a state of impasse, because Puccini's real passion in life was his music – and it's on Puccini the musician that I've concentrated.

Note

The casts at the first performance of each opera are shown, but unfortunately there is no record of the names or complete names of the singers who played some of the minor roles.

Operatic Terms

I've kept the use of operatic terms to a minimum in this book because too many of them can make readers feel that they've come in on the middle of somebody else's conversation.

'Aria' is used quite often and most people will probably know that it's the Italian equivalent of 'air' or 'song' – and is a solo passage in an opera. Puccini's 'Nessun dorma' is an aria that became popular when the BBC used it to introduce their World Cup programmes in 1990. A short solo is called an 'arietta' – a small aria.

'Arioso' is a long, solo passage which isn't as tuneful as an aria, but when it's particularly dramatic it's called 'recitative' – which is very like its English equivalent, recital.

'Parlando' – which means 'spoken' – is the ordinary sung dialogue in an opera.

'Libretto' – which means 'small book' or 'booklet' – is the text of an opera, like the screenplay of a film. Composers like Puccini would decide on a story that they could adapt into an opera, then engage a writer to provide the libretto.

The composer and the librettist would first work out the structure of the opera – how many acts there should be and how the action should be divided into them – then the librettist would start to write. When the libretto was complete, the composer would set it to music, although sometimes, when it took a long time, he would work on parts of it, acts or scenes, as they were written.

Puccini often used two librettists, one to make the story into a play with lines for the various characters, the other to convert the lines into verse dialogue, more suitable for singing.

The completion of the libretti for some of Puccini's best-known operas was often a story in itself, with many disagreements between him and the librettists occurring, often because he was apt to change his mind about how the opera should proceed as he went along. That extended what would in any case have been a long and complicated process. If the long and difficult task of producing a libretto is understood from the start, it's easier to understand why Puccini's way of going about things often made that task even longer and more difficult.

I

Beginnings

The operas of Puccini are set in a number of countries – France, Japan, America, China, as well his native Italy – but they all had their origins in the small Tuscan town of Lucca. It was in Lucca, on 22 December 1858, that Giacomo Antonio Domenico Michele Secondo Maria Puccini was born – the fifth of the seven children born to Michele Puccini, organist choirmaster of the cathedral of San Martino and his wife, Albina.

The Puccini family came to Lucca when Giacomo's great-great-grandfather, also Giacomo, brought them there from Celle in the Apuan Alps, where he was born in 1712. The Puccinis were soon established as a musical family and composed short operas and cantatas for local festivals, and Michele, Giacomo's father, taught music at the town's Istituto Musicale Pacini before he took up his post at the cathedral. He died in 1864 and Giacomo, then only five, had already shown such a talent for music that when his uncle, Fortunato Magi, took over his post, a clause in his contract stipulated that he would hand it over to his nephew 'as soon as the said Signore Giacomo is able to discharge such duties'.

Puccini was a choirboy at the age of ten and when he was fourteen he played the organ at the cathedral and at churches in some of the neighbouring villages. To make some money for the family he also played the piano at local taverns and, it's believed, at a brothel. Addicted to smoking – probably the eventual cause of his death – at an early age, he used some of his earnings to buy cigarettes and the short cigars called Toscanos which were popular in that part of Tuscany. He also raised money to support his habit by stealing organ pipes from the cathedral and selling them. The theft would remain undiscovered because he was already dextrous enough as a musician to avoid using the missing notes when he next played the organ.

This was strange behaviour for a boy whose family had strong Church connections – he was obviously not above stealing and could have had no reverence for the Church – and it was an indication of his character and his approach to life. When Puccini wanted something, he instinctively moved towards it – usually regardless of the consequences. It was just as well that he never did become the choirmaster at the cathedral because, soon after the death of his mother in July 1884, he set up house with Elvira Gemignani, a married woman with two children who had once been his musical pupil. If it was in deference to Albina that he did not do so during her lifetime, it would have been one of the few concessions to the opinions or feelings of others that he ever made.

As he probably realised, Puccini owed a great deal to his mother. He had his first lessons in music from his uncle Fortunato, Albina's brother, but made better progress when she found him another teacher at the Pacini Institute. Magi's way of reprimanding any of his choirboys who sang a wrong note was to give him a kick in the shins – and it was said that in later years, when he was watching rehearsals of his operas, Puccini would give an involuntary twitch of his lower leg if one of his singers ever failed to reach a note. Perhaps his uncle had been particularly hard on him because he was required to make way for him when Puccini was considered to be old enough for the post.

Puccini's new teacher was Carlo Angeloni, who had been one of Michele Puccini's students. It was Angeloni who first introduced Puccini to opera when he showed him some Verdi scores, perhaps realising that it was in that direction that his talents would be better directed. He certainly succeeded in arousing his interest, because in March 1876 Puccini was so anxious to see a performance of Verdi's

Aida in Pisa that he walked 20 miles from Lucca, together with his brother Michele and some friends whom he had persuaded to join him.

'I felt that a musical window had opened for me,' was how he later described his reaction to the experience that proved to be the turning point of his career. He had already begun to compose organ music, but after seeing *Aida* he began to turn to other works. Like his ancestors he produced music for local religious festivals, which brought him to the notice of the local press and greatly impressed Angeloni. In later years he used some of the music that he composed at that time in his operas – which his critics referred to as 'self-plagiarism'.

Puccini completed his studies at the Pacini Institute when he was twenty-one and he took the next step to becoming an operatic composer by sitting the entrance examination to the Milan Conservatorium. He passed without any difficulty but then had the problem of finding finance for a three-year stay in Milan. He received no help at all from the mayor or the council and local ecclesiastical authorities, no doubt because they felt that he should have stayed in Lucca and taken up the post of choirmaster which had been guaranteed for him when his father died. The problem was solved for him by Albina, who was completely undeterred by the fact that if he went to Milan she would lose the money that he earned for the family from his various activities in Lucca. Firstly, she addressed a petition to Queen Margherita of Italy for Puccini to be granted one of the scholarships that the Queen was awarding to musicians from needy families. Then, when it was agreed that Puccini should benefit but only for one year, Albina approached her uncle, Nicalau Cerú, a doctor and part-time columnist for a local newspaper. Cerú had been impressed by his great-nephew's musical works and gladly agreed to guarantee him for the remaining two years.

In Milan, Puccini shared lodgings with Pietro Mascagni, who also became an operatic composer but was limited to only one real success, his one-act opera *Cavalleria Rusticana*. They lived as typical students, incurring debts and existing on a shoestring. When Puccini's creditors called, he would hide and Mascagni would tell them that he was out. When Mascagni cooked meals, which was the cheapest way to eat but forbidden in their lodgings, Puccini would play the piano loudly to drown the sound of the cooking. Once, when he had invited a young dancer out for dinner, Puccini had to pawn his coat so that he could pay for the meal.

Puccini's two main teachers at the Conservatorium were Antonio Bazzini and Amilcare Ponchielli. Bazzini, formerly a violin virtuoso, had composed an opera, *Turanda*, based on a story by Carlo Gozzi which was the basis for Puccini's final opera *Turandot*, premiered in 1926. Ponchielli was also an operatic composer but, like Mascagni, he produced only one work that had any real success. This was *La Giaconda*, first staged in 1876, and now chiefly remembered for its tenor aria 'Cielo e mar' ('Heaven and sea') which is still a concert favourite, and for its ballet music the 'Dance of the Hours'. Ponchielli continued to take an interest in Puccini when he had left the Conservatorium and encouraged him to compose his first opera, *Le Villi*.

Puccini left the Conservatorium in 1883. A student completing his studies was required to pass his final examination by composing a 'finishing exercise' and Puccini's was not a vocal piece as might have been expected but an orchestral work, *Capriccio Sinfonico*. It was played by the student orchestra, on that occasion under the baton of the leading operatic conductor Franco Faccio, and favourably reviewed by Filippo Filippi, one of Italy's influential critics. Faccio conducted it on two more occasions but those were its only performances. Later in his career, Puccini used parts of it in two of his operas and it was probably for that reason that he refused to have it published. Had he done so, it would have been played again and the 'self-plagiarism' would have been obvious.

Having received his diploma from the conservatorium, Puccini could still have returned to Lucca and taken up his promised post of choirmaster at the cathedral, or he could have accepted an offer to teach at the Pacini Institute. Instead, he decided to stay in Milan and pursue his ambition to become an operatic composer. As we know, he succeeded, but it's interesting to speculate whether it would have happened if his father had not died when Puccini was still a child.

Would a father's control have restricted his activities and given him a narrower perspective on life and consequently a narrower ambition? It seems unlikely because Puccini's talent was inborn and somehow or other would almost certainly have found its outlet. The impulsive nature that as an adolescent led him to fund his smoking habit by selling stolen organ pipes, and as an adult to indulge in many affairs with women, must also have been inborn. It's difficult to imagine him accepting life as a provincial choirmaster which, whenever Michele had died, would probably have been Puccini's ultimate existence.

2

Le Villi

Libretto by Ferdinando Fontana
Based on 'Les Willis', a short story by Jean-Baptiste Alphonse-Karr

Premiere – Teatro dal Verme, Milan, 31 May 1884
Conductor – Achille Panizza

CAST

Guglielmo Wulf, a forester	Baritone	Erminio Peltz
Anna Wulf, his daughter	Soprano	Rosina Caponetti
Roberto, betrothed to Anna	Tenor	Antonio D'Andrade

Puccini's first published opera, *Le Villi*, was written for a competition instituted by Edoardo Sonzogno (1836–1920), a Milan publisher. On the death of Edoardo's father he turned the family printing business into a publishing firm, the Casa Sonzogno, which opened in 1874. The competition, called the Sonzogno Prize, was to encourage young operatic composers and was for one-act operas. The most famous opera to win it was Mascagni's *Cavalleria Rusticana*, which he submitted in 1889 and was performed in 1890.

Puccini, having completed his studies at the Milan Conservatorium, decided to enter for the prize in 1883. His former teacher Amilcare Ponchielli found a librettist for him and this was Ferdinando Fontana, a journalist and a writer of plays and poetry. In later years he translated two of Franz Lehár's operettas, *The Merry Widow* and *The Count of Luxemburg*, for performance in Italy. The opera they produced was *Le Villi*, based on a German folk legend of the 'Willi' – the spirits of jilted maidens who return to take revenge on their betrayers by making them dance with them until they die of exhaustion. The story of *Le Villi* was similar to that of the ballet *Giselle*.

The opera failed to win the competition or to even gain a place, and it has been suggested that this was because the score was illegible. Puccini's writing was usually bad and was probably worse in this instance because he had had to hurry to meet the deadline for entries, which was 31 December 1883. Fontana, however, was not willing for their efforts to be wasted and, being older and more experienced than Puccini, he took the initiative in promoting the work.

As a journalist, he knew the value of contacts and he had an acquaintance who often entertained well-known writers and musicians at his home. He arranged for Puccini to be present at one of their gatherings to play excerpts from the opera. It was through this that Puccini came to the notice of the influential Milan publisher Giulio Ricordi, who agreed to publish a free edition of *Le Villi*. Puccini found another valuable supporter in Arrigo Boito, who had written the libretto of Verdi's *Simon Boccanegra*. He funded the first performance of *Le Villi*, staged at the Teatro dal Verme in Milan, in May 1884. Pietro Mascagni, Puccini's friend from his student days, was in the contrabass section of the orchestra on that significant occasion.

After the performance, Puccini sent a telegram to Albina reading, 'Theatre packed, immense success; anticipations exceeded; eighteen calls; finale of first act encored thrice.'

With Puccini already having attracted powerful support from luminaries like Boito and Ponchielli, the premiere was well covered by the press and one reviewer referred to him as 'one of the most brilliant and promising hopes of art'. Albina, who died six weeks later, would have been happy to think that her earlier efforts had helped her son on the way to a successful career.

For the premiere, Puccini had adapted *Le Villi* into a two-act opera, which was a logical move as the action was divided into two distinct phases. It was still a very short work, however, and is rarely staged because of the difficulty in finding another suitably short opera to present with it as a double bill – at the Teatro dal Verme it was actually one of three operas that were performed on the night of the premiere – but it has been regularly recorded and a new version was released as recently as 2004. Three recordings were made in 1979, including one in which the great tenor Plácido Domingo sang the lead.

The story is a simple one, set in a village in the Black Forest in the middle ages. Anna, daughter of Guglielmo Wulf, a forester, has just become betrothed to Roberto, but he is about to leave her for a while to go to Mainz, to collect an inheritance. Anna is sad about this, and when operatic heroines have forebodings, they usually have a good reason. Roberto goes off amid prayers for his safety and swift return from the villagers, and with Gugliemo's blessing, but in Mainz he becomes infatuated with a 'temptress' and does not return for some time. Anna hopefully waits for him through the summer and autumn but when the winter comes on she dies.

Guglielmo blames Roberto for his daughter's death and, knowing the legend of the Villi, invokes them to bring retribution on him and they call on the ghost of Anna to lure him into the forest if he returns. Roberto does come back, when the news of Anna's death reaches him. The 'temptress' has lost interest in him and, no doubt because she has helped him to spend his inheritance, he is penniless.

The Villi prevent him from trying to knock on the door of Gugliemo's house and when he tries to pray for forgiveness he is prevented by a curse that they have put on him. As he bemoans his fate, Anna appears to him and tells him of her sufferings. Telling Anna that he also has felt her pain, he begs her to forgive him, but she and the Villi dance with him until he falls dead from exhaustion at her feet. Anna and the Villi depart with a triumphant shout of 'Hosanna!'

Puccini ended the first act with the departure of Roberto, which provides a suitable finale as Guglielmo leads the villagers in their prayers for him. It was, as Puccini said in his telegram to Albina, enthusiastically received with three encores. Between the two acts there was an orchestral intermezzo, in which the audience are told of Roberto deserting Anna and the Villi calling on her spirit to take revenge on him. This is done with verses, usually spoken by a narrator. It's believed that Fontana thought the audience should read the verses – presumably in the programme – while Puccini thought they should be recited. After the intermezzo the second act begins with Roberto's return to the village and ends with Anna's vengeance.

As he did throughout his career, Puccini provided arias and duets for the principals. Anna sings 'Se come voi piccina' ('If I were like you, my little darling'), telling Roberto of her fear that she will never see him again, whereupon he reassures her, and when she says that she has dreams of him dying he tells her that she may doubt her God but not his love for her. Apart from leading the prayers for Roberto in Act 1, Guglielmo has the aria 'Anima santa della figlia mia' ('Holy spirit of my daughter') calling on the Villi to avenge Anna. When the now desolate Roberto returns to the village he regrets the loss of his happy youth – 'Torna ai felici dì' ('Return, days of happiness'). These pieces are rarely included in record albums or sung in concert but the fairly regular recording of complete versions of *Le Villi* makes it possible for them to still be heard.

The year 1884 saw the beginning of Puccini's career as a composer and also of another phase in his life. He had been having an affair with Elvira Gemignani, the wife of a merchant in Lucca, and later that year, after the death of Albina, she left her husband and set up house with Puccini. Elvira and her husband had two children: a son who stayed with his father and a daughter, Fosca, whom Elvira took with her to live with Puccini. In Roman Catholic Italy in the nineteenth century, this was naturally regarded as outrageous behaviour, and with their strong Church connections it must have greatly embarrassed the Puccini family. Nicalau Cerú, Puccini's great uncle who had financed his last two years of study at Milan, wrote to him, telling him that if he could afford a mistress, he could afford to repay the money to him.

It seems, however, that Puccini and Elvira were prepared to accept this disapproval, and probably a lot of open hostility, as long as they could be together. Their only concession to local opinion was when Elvira became pregnant the following year and they left Lucca for Monza, near Milan. It's strange, therefore, that despite their obvious devotion to each other, Puccini had affairs with many different women throughout his career. In seeking a reason for that, his biographers have advanced various theories, sometimes delving into the psychological.

The respected Austrian-born musicologist Mosco Carner (1904–85) suggested that when Puccini's father died and Albina became the dominant figure in his life, he harboured incestuous thoughts about her, causing him to have guilt feelings. Having an affair with Elvira might have assuaged them at first, but when they were living together, practically as man and wife and accepted as such by their friends, it became almost respectable and was no longer sufficient. Consequently, he pursued other women, usually his intellectual and social inferiors.

This may be a valid theory but there could be a much less complicated explanation, particularly as there is no certainty that Puccini had incestuous feeling about his mother. As he became successful as a composer he was often away from home, overseeing rehearsals and productions, in Italy and in various other countries. With a large Italian community in Argentina, there was an audience for his operas there. With all this travelling there would have been many opportunities for affairs and, as he had demonstrated during his 'wild-child' formative years in Lucca, Puccini could be quite undeterred by moral considerations in matters of physical pleasure.

It's likely that Elvira suspected that Puccini was often unfaithful to her but turned a blind eye, and in the letters that he sent to her there is evidence of a deep and lasting affection between them that made his affairs incidental. Years later, his philandering was to have tragic consequences, but in 1884, having come together with his real love and apparently heading for success as a composer, a blissful future for Puccini seemed assured. As far as his musical future was concerned, he was soon to find that the path would not be as smooth as he might have thought, but *Le Villi* had been the first step and probably the most important one.

3

Edgar

Libretto by Ferdinando Fontana
Based on *La Coupe et les Lèvres* by Alfred de Musset

Premiere – Teatro della Scala, Milan, 21 April 1889
Conductor – Franco Faccio

CAST

Edgar	Tenor	Gregorio Gabrielesco
Fidelia	Soprano	Aurelia Cattaneo
Tigrana	Mezzo-Soprano	Romilda Pantaleoni
Frank	Baritone	Antonio Magini-Coletti
Gualtiero	Bass	Pio Marini

Puccini's second opera, *Edgar*, was based on the verse play *La Coupe et les Lèvres* by the French writer Alfred de Musset. The title meant 'The Cup and the Lips', a play on the saying, 'Many a slip ...' – and for Puccini it was appropriate. He had had a minor triumph with *Le Villi*, which had brought him to the notice of Giulio Ricordi, and he probably expected that *Edgar* would be another success for him. Ricordi must have shared his confidence because he had the opera premiered at La Scala, Milan, the Mecca of Italian opera, which no doubt increased Puccini's embarrassment when it was a failure.

It was Fontana who wrote the libretto for *Edgar*, as he had for *Le Villi*, and who suggested that the de Musset play was suitable for an opera. Puccini may have allowed himself to be persuaded because he was grateful to Fontana for persevering with *Le Villi* and introducing his work to Ricordi. The failure of the piece was probably the reason that for a long time afterwards he was ultra-cautious in his selection of themes for his operas, and even when he had begun work on one he was always likely to change his mind about its form and structure. Originally, *Edgar* was written in four acts but Puccini changed it to three, which the action divided into quite naturally. With that and other difficulties that he had with Fontana's libretto, it took him three years to complete the opera.

Edgar is set in Flanders, in 1302, and opens in the village where the hero Edgar lives. He is betrothed to Fidelia but still has feelings for his former lover Tigrana, a gypsy girl. Tigrana was originally the only full-length part that Puccini ever wrote for a mezzo-soprano, but he shortened it in an adapted version. When Tigrana is attacked by some peasants for singing a suggestive song as they pray outside the church, Edgar defends her, then sets fire to his family home and elopes with her. Frank, Fidelia's brother who also is in love with Tigrana, tries to stop them. He and Edgar fight and he is wounded. Edgar and Tigrana go off, but Edgar soon regrets his action.

In the second act he has been living a life of debauchery with Tigrana at her home, and as basically a very moral character he is becoming uncomfortable with it. He meets Frank with some soldiers and the two men are instantly reconciled. To Tigrana's fury, Edgar goes off with Frank, determined to reconcile his honour in battle. She curses the two men and swears to take her revenge on them as they go off with the soldiers.

In the final act, Frank and a hooded monk bring in a body in full armour and place it on a catafalque. They say it is Edgar, who has been killed in battle. Fidelia is there to mourn her love and has to defend him when the monk reminds the onlookers of how Edgar burnt down his house and went off to follow a life of debauchery, and they are about to throw his body 'to the crows'. When a tearful Tigrana comes to mourn Edgar, Frank and the monk manage to bribe her to join them in accusations that he was about to betray his country 'for gold'. The assembled soldiers take the body from the catafalque, only to find that the armour is empty and the monk then reveals that he is Edgar. He embraces Fidelia, who is promptly stabbed by Tigrana. As Edgar falls weeping on her body, the soldiers take Tigrana away to be executed.

Modern analysts, and particularly feminist ones, would probably feel that Edgar and Frank were both anxious to blame Tigrana for their own folly in their associations with her and that this was the reason for their rather ludicrous charade in the final act. She could well have been genuine in the grief that she displayed when she thought that Edgar was dead – Carmen, the operatic character to whom she is often likened, would not even have bothered to pretend, as she had little time for Don José after she had lured him away from his virtuous sweetheart Micaëla. Tigrana's two former lovers were, it seems, anxious to present her in as bad a light as possible, and if Fidelia hadn't paid the price, we might feel that Edgar got all he deserved.

Edgar received only one complimentary notice in the press, and after Puccini had spent some time trying to improve it, Ricordi called him and Fontana in to discuss the situation. Afterwards, he wrote a long letter to Puccini. He signalled his feelings on the matter by first pointing out that it was the composer who was the all-important person in the production of an opera. He then went on to say that he did not agree with the 'systematic belittlers' of Fontana's libretto but, while he felt that it contained two effective acts, 'It also contains much obscurity, many fallacies which derive from the theories of Fontana, who assumes that everyone thinks with his head.'

From their discussion, he said, he was certain that Fontana would 'never benefit from the experience of these days' and he felt that before Puccini made any more attempt to improve the opera, 'it is necessary that I talk to you alone'.

Ricordi's message was clear. The opera had failed because of the libretto and Fontana would never produce anything better because he was unwilling to listen to criticism. On Ricordi's advice, Puccini began to look for a theme for a new opera but when there were later productions of *Edgar* he often made alterations in the hope that he might improve it. This went on until 1905 when he attended a performance in Buenos Aires and wrote home to Elvira saying, 'It is warmed up soup. I have always said so.'

His complete disenchantment with the piece was shown some years later when he gave a copy of the score to a close friend, Sybil Seligman, an English woman who was married to a wealthy banker in London. Puccini met Mrs Seligman in 1904 and it's generally accepted that, at first, their relationship was a sexual one – nobody who knew him would have expected anything else – but in later years she became important to him as a person to whom he could express himself in a way that was never possible with Elvira.

Mrs Seligman came of a family that had a great interest in music and she herself had a good contralto voice. She sometimes advised him on his choice of stories for his operas when they were in the preparatory stage. They were constant companions whenever he was in London, often going to the theatre together, and as Puccini had convinced the usually jealous Elvira that their friendship was a purely intellectual one, she and her family often visited him in Italy. Puccini exchanged numerous letters with her and in 1938 a collection of over 700 letters that he had sent to her was published by her elder son Vincent, under the title *Puccini Among Friends*. It was carefully edited so that there was no suggestion that their relationship had been anything more than a platonic friendship of like minds, but it still contained some of the clearest and most interesting insights into Puccini's thinking and character that have ever emerged.

On the copy of *Edgar* that Puccini sent to Mrs Seligman he altered the title to read 'E Dio ti GARdi da quest' opera' – meaning 'and may God protect you from this opera'. He also added comments at various places on the score, one of them describing the finale to the second act as 'The most horrible thing ever written.' Where Edgar removes the monk's cowl and dramatically tells Fidelia 'Yes, Edgar lives', he wrote 'Mesogna!' ('It's a lie!'). And when Tigrana stabs Fidelia and the crowd murmur 'Horror! Horror!' he commented 'How right they are!'

There were, however, two parts of the score that he did look back upon without embarrassment and these were two arias sung by Fidelia in Act 3. Against both of them he wrote, 'This is good.' One of them was 'In Edgar's village I too was born', which Fidelia sings as she defends her lover against the hostile crowd. The other, 'Goodbye, goodbye my sweet love', was actually sung at Puccini's funeral in 1924, at Toscanini's suggestion. Fidelia sings this when what she believes to be Edgar's body is placed on the catafalque.

If Puccini had felt at all complacent after *Le Villi* had gained him recognition as a composer, *Edgar* taught him a valuable lesson; and whether or not he realised it, the failure may have come near to ending his career. He was then living on royalties from *Le Villi* and a small allowance from Ricordi and the failure of *Edgar* prompted the publisher's business associates to urge him to end his patronage of Puccini. The reason for that was quite possibly hypocritical. It was widely known that Puccini and Elvira were 'living in sin', and by the time that *Edgar* was first performed they had a son, Tonio, who was born in 1886. Ricordi's colleagues were probably prepared to ignore this while he seemed to be on the brink of a successful career and therefore a good investment for them. When his second opera failed, however, it might have persuaded some of them that *Le Villi* had been a false dawn and that consequently it was time to end this embarrassing association with him.

Ricordi resisted these demands and actually threatened to resign from the firm if the others had their way. He insisted that Puccini should continue to receive his allowance from them and promised to personally refund the firm if the investment did not ultimately prove to be a profitable one. Fortunately for both of them Puccini took his advice and, although there were later performances of *Edgar*, he gave up trying to improve it and began to look for a new subject. As it usually did, Ricordi's advice proved to be sound, and possibly because he knew how much he owed the publisher, Puccini always gave his opinions the utmost respect. His 'Papa Giulio', as he often called the publisher, was one of the few people whose criticisms of his work he would accept.

4

Manon Lescaut

Libretto by Ruggero Leoncavallo, Domenico Oliva, Marco Praga, Giuseppe Giacosa and Luigi Illica
Based on *L'histoire du chevalier des Grieux et de Manon Lescaut* by the Abbé Prévost

Premiere – Teatro Regio, Turin, 1 February 1893
Conductor – Alessandro Pomè

CAST

Manon Lescaut	Soprano	Cesira Ferrani
Chevalier des Grieux	Tenor	Giuseppe Cremonini
Geronte de Ravoir	Bass	Alessandro Polonini
Edmondo, a student	Tenor	Roberto Ramini
Innkeeper	Bass	Augusto Castagnola
Singer	Mezzo-Soprano	Elvira Ceresoli
Dancing Master	Tenor	Roberto Ramini
Lamplighter	Tenor	Roberto Ramini
Sergeant of Royal Archers	Bass	Ferdin Cattadori
Naval Captain	Bass	
Hairdresser	Silent	Augusto Ghinghini

When Puccini began work on his third opera, *Manon Lescaut*, he and Elvira had left Monza, where they had gone to live when Elvira had become pregnant, and after a brief return to Lucca they had taken up residence in Torre del Lago, a village on Lake Massociuccoli, near Viareggio. With them were their son Tonio, then three, and Elvira's daughter Fosca, whom she had taken with her when she left her husband. *Manon Lescaut* was of great importance in Puccini's career for two reasons. It was his first major success and, completely by chance, it brought together the two librettists who collaborated with him on his most popular operas, *La Bohème*, *Tosca* and *Madama Butterfly*.

Giulio Ricordi persuaded Puccini to stop trying to make alterations to *Edgar* to make it a success and to move on to something entirely new. He engaged Giuseppe Giacosa, a well-respected poet and playwright, to write a libretto for Puccini and Giacosa began work on one, based on a Russian story. Puccini would have been pleased to have the collaboration of a man of Giacosa's ability and reputation but he decided the story was not suitable for his music. Possibly he recognised that the failure of *Edgar* might have ended his career and, knowing that he badly needed a success, he was not going to take any chances with his next effort.

He told Ricordi that he would find his own story and after a short while he decided on *L'histoire du chevalier des Grieux et de Manon Lescaut*, a short novel by the Abbé Prévost, a monk and later a writer in the eighteenth century. Ricordi accepted the idea reluctantly because the story had also been used for an opera, *Manon*, by the French composer Massenet, twelve years earlier – Puccini's was titled *Manon Lescaut* to differentiate it. Neither Puccini nor Ricordi could have known that there had already been an opera of that title which was written by the French composer Daniel Auber in 1856.

Puccini was not put off at all by the fact that there had already been an opera about his heroine, and asked, 'Why shouldn't there be two operas about Manon? A woman like Manon can have more than one lover.' The character of his heroine was often a big factor when he chose the themes of his operas and he said that Manon 'cannot fail to win the hearts of the public'.

When he began to compose the opera, Puccini decided to write his own libretto. The failure of *Edgar* and its near disastrous consequences for him were obviously on his mind when he said that this time he was not going to let 'any idiotic librettist' spoil things for him. Ricordi, however, persuaded him to let the composer Leoncavallo write the libretto. Leoncavallo, who in 1892 had had what was to be his only real success with his two-act opera *Pagliacci*, wrote his own libretti but it was not long before Puccini decided that their thinking was too unalike and he asked Ricordi to end their association.

Instead of reverting to the idea of writing his own libretto, Puccini approached Marco Praga, who was beginning a successful career as a playwright. Praga was surprised by this as he had never previously been involved in the production of an opera, which might well have been why Puccini approached him. With Praga having no experience, the opera could be constructed completely in accordance with Puccini's wishes. Praga said that he was willing to write the libretto but felt that he would be unable to provide the verses that were so important in an opera. Puccini felt that that should create no difficulty – Praga could find a suitable collaborator to contribute that part of the libretto and he would accept his choice. Praga enlisted his close friend Domenico Oliva, who had just published a highly acclaimed book of poems.

The three men set to work. Writing about it in later years, Praga said that the libretto was completed quite quickly, with everyone happy with it, but Puccini then began to have doubts. He asked Praga to make alterations, some of them quite radical, and this went on until Praga became completely frustrated and, feeling that he could no longer keep up with Puccini's constant changes of mind, he walked out on the project. Oliva was left to complete the libretto, which he was reluctant to do on his own, and when Puccini continued to insist on changes, he decided he too had had enough and withdrew. In his correspondence with Ricordi, Puccini had been critical of Oliva's work so he would not have been too worried by his departure, except that he then had no librettist to complete his opera.

All this vacillation was probably due, at least in part, to Puccini's experience with *Edgar* and it remained a facet of his composing for some years to come. In this instance, it left him with a libretto that was not merely incomplete but in a state of flux, and Ricordi was forced to come to his rescue. He approached Giacosa, but only to ask for his advice. It was not all that long ago that Puccini had rejected the libretto that Giacosa had begun for him and Ricordi probably felt that some tact was needed. Had he been asked directly to collaborate on *Manon Lescaut*, as Ricordi would probably have liked, Giacosa might have retorted that Puccini had turned down his work before and might only be prepared to accept it now because there was no one else to turn to.

It's possible that Giacosa did have some such thoughts because he made no offer to help but suggested that Ricordi should approach another playwright, Luigi Illica. Like Giacosa, Illica had musical experience, with his most notable work being the libretto for Alfredo Catalani's successful opera *La Wally*, premiered at La Scala in 1892. Ricordi took this advice and later, when Illica had begun work on the libretto, Giacosa also became involved. When they began working together, the two men formed an ideal partnership. As a playwright himself, Giacosa could follow Illica's thinking and as a poet he supplied a lyrical touch and wrote the all-important verses.

Ricordi was also an important member of what became a most successful team. He actually contributed some of the verses for *Manon Lescaut* but most importantly he held the others together in the difficult moments that sometimes arose and used his theatrical experience to make suggestions about the validity of situations created within the plot. With Ricordi guiding them, Puccini, Illica and Giacosa went on to produce three highly acclaimed and still frequently performed operas.

With disagreements sometimes arising, it was probably fortunate that Puccini and his librettists worked separately. Illica and Giacosa would complete their own parts of the work, then send them on to Puccini for him to set them to music. There were times when they kept him waiting when he was anxious to press on and he often expressed his impatience and frustration in letters to friends like

Sybil Seligman. The lack of personal contact, however, gave him time to think about any criticisms that he felt necessary, which probably avoided even more friction than frequently arose between him and the librettists.

Manon Lescaut was completed in the autumn of 1892 and first performed in February of the following year. With so many of them having been involved in the production of the opera, no librettists were named on the original score and Ricordi may still have had doubts about the finished piece. He chose the Teatro Regio in Turin as the venue for that first performance, perhaps because he was unwilling to risk another failure for Puccini at La Scala, where *Edgar* had its premiere. If that was his feeling, he worried unnecessarily. *Manon Lescaut* was an instant success, with Puccini and the cast sharing some thirty curtain calls at the end. Press comment was enthusiastic and after its London premiere in 1894 George Bernard Shaw, then the music critic of *The World*, commented that, to him, Puccini 'looked more like the heir to Verdi [for many years Italy's leading operatic composer] than any of his rivals'.

Manon Lescaut has four acts, the first of which is set in the square of the small French town of Amiens, in the evening. Des Grieux, the hero, his friend Edmundo and their fellow students are talking together and trying to attract the attention of some of the local girls. A coach arrives from Arras and stops by the local inn, where some of the passengers decide to stay for the night. These include Geronte de Ravoir, a rich and elderly Treasurer General, and Lescaut, a sergeant in the King's Guard, who is taking his young sister Manon to a convent. As he later confides to Geronte, he feels it a shame that a girl still in her teens should be sent to be a nun, but as a soldier he is used to obeying orders and feels it his duty to carry out his family's instructions.

When Lescaut and Geronte go into the inn to arrange their accommodation, Des Grieux meets Manon and instantly falls in love with her. Geronte also has designs on her, however, and tells the innkeeper to bring a coach to the door so that he can take her off to Paris with him. Edmundo overhears this and warns Des Grieux, then calls the other students to help them. They distract Lescaut by inviting him to drink with them, and when Geronte's coach arrives Des Grieux persuades Manon to escape in it with him and they go off to Paris. Geronte's instinct is to go after them but Lescaut dissuades him. There would be no chance of catching them and from Geronte's point of view it would be unnecessary. Manon, young and pleasure-loving, will soon tire of life with a penniless student and then the advances of a rich Treasurer General will be irresistible. Geronte sees the logic of this and the act ends with the two men going into the inn to take their supper.

When the second act opens, Lescaut's prediction has been fulfilled. Manon is comfortably installed in Geronte's house in Paris, with servants attending her. Lescaut, who has helped to lure her away from Des Grieux, comes in and finds her in a strangely distracted mood, hardly acknowledging it when he compliments her on her beauty. After a while, she confides in him that the elderly Geronte is beginning to bore her and asks him about Des Grieux. Lescaut tells her that her former lover has taken up gambling in the hope that he might win a lot of money and tempt her away from Geronte. We gather from this that, although he is still besotted with her, Des Grieux is all too aware of Manon's real priorities in life.

The act continues with some musicians coming to entertain Manon with a madrigal composed by Geronte. Puccini used music from several of his earlier works in the opera and the madrigal was based on part of a 'Mass for Four Voices' that he had written in 1880. Geronte then arrives with some guests. Manon is given a dancing lesson, after which she pleases Geronte by singing a cantata. She is, in fact, hoping this jollity will bring about a change in her mood. Perhaps because he now regrets helping Geronte to separate the young lovers, Lescaut goes off to find Des Grieux.

Geronte and his friends leave and Des Grieux arrives. At first he reproaches Manon for leaving him but then tells her how much he still loves her. Manon responds to him and they are in each other's arms when Geronte suddenly returns. Having finally realised where her true affections lie, Manon refuses to excuse her behaviour to him and when she taunts him he walks out in fury. Manon is pleased to see him but when Des Grieux urges her to leave she is reluctant as it will mean giving up the comfortable life that she has been enjoying.

Lescaut comes in to warn them that Geronte has reported Manon to the police as an immoral woman and is on his way with some guards to have her arrested. She and Des Grieux try to escape but are caught because she insists on collecting up all her jewellery before she will leave. When Des Grieux draws his sword intending to defend her, Lescaut stops him. He points out that if he also is arrested there will be nobody to rescue Manon, who is then dragged away. Des Grieux attempts to follow her but Lescaut restrains him.

The third act takes place in Le Havre, outside a barracks where Manon is being held before she and some prostitutes are deported to the then French colony of Louisiana. Lescaut and Des Grieux have a plan to rescue Manon and have bribed a sentry to allow Des Grieux to speak to her through the barred window of the barracks. Lescaut goes off to start the rescue operation, but after the sound of a rifle shot from offstage he returns to tell them that something has gone wrong and their plan has failed.

The captain of the ship which is to take the women to Louisiana arrives with his crew and one by one they come out as their names are called. With Manon among them, they go off to the ship while the local people jeer at them. Des Grieux persuades the captain to let him go with her as a cabin boy. He goes off after her and the watching Lescaut sadly walks away.

The fourth and final act is a short one, in which Manon and Des Grieux are the only characters involved. The setting is a barren waste outside New Orleans, at nightfall. Manon and Des Grieux appear, ragged and almost exhausted. After a happy start in America, they have found further misfortune because Manon has attracted a new admirer, the nephew of the governor of the colony, and Des Grieux fought a duel with him. This ends with his rival unconscious but Des

Grieux believes that he is dead and he and Manon have fled together and are now destitute. Des Grieux goes off to find some water for Manon but when he returns she is barely conscious. Having assured him of her love, she dies and he collapses beside her, presumably soon to die himself.

We are shown none of the action which has brought them to their plight. It is merely suggested by the line 'They wanted to tear me from him' from an aria that Manon sings when Des Grieux has left her in the desert. As critics have pointed out, we could only know what really happened by referring to the original story by Prévost. To have shown Des Grieux fighting the duel would have added to the action, but it would have meant another scene or even an additional act. In the tortuous process from which the libretto finally evolved, this may have been considered; but if it was, it was probably decided against because by the time Illica and Giacosa finally became involved, completion of the opera was becoming a matter of urgency.

Theatrically, it might have been better to have left out the Le Havre episode and set the third act in Louisiana, with the presence there of Manon and Des Grieux explained. The duel between Des Grieux and Manon's admirer could then have been shown as the climax of the act. The final act would then have followed more logically; but as it stands, it's still effective. Some would say that it was what became a traditional Puccinian ending, in which the heroine suffers a tragic and moving death. If that last sequence seemed confusing at the premiere it hardly mattered because by then the success of the opera was assured. Early in the first act an aria sung by Des Grieux was greeted with great enthusiasm and Puccini was called on stage to acknowledge the applause.

Des Grieux has two arias in the first act. The first, which drew the applause at the premiere, is 'Tra voi belle' (Among you, beautiful ones dark and fair, is there a maiden coy and tender, whose lips so rosy will kisses render?). It's a light-hearted piece, sung in response to some banter from the assembled students when they see Des Grieux apparently in a melancholy mood. 'Tra voi Belle' and the second aria

'Donna non vidi mai' ('I have never seen such a lady before') – sung by Des Grieux when he has first seen Manon – were both included in Pavarotti's concert in Hyde Park in 1991, attended by the Prince and Princess of Wales. He dedicated 'Donna non vidi mai' to 'the lady Diana'. It's a short but beautiful aria, the theme of which is repeated at significant points in the opera. Although the setting is the French town of Amiens, it is very Italian in character.

In his first opera, *Le Villi*, Puccini gave an appropriately Germanic sound to one aria. Debussy said that he knew of nobody who had 'described the Paris of that time as well as Puccini in *La Bohème*'. A later opera, *Fanciulla del West*, set in the Californian gold rush, is full of American-sounding themes, and *Madama Butterfly* and *Turandot* – stories of Japan and China – are brilliantly suffused with oriental sounds. 'Donna non vidi mai', however, is instantly reminiscent of a small town in Puccini's native Tuscany – but that should spoil nobody's enjoyment of it.

Des Grieux has another solo, 'Guardate, pazzo son' ('See I am mad') in Act 3, when Manon is led away to the ship. This is purely a part of the opera and as it doesn't 'stand alone' it isn't one of Puccini's arias that's often heard on the concert platform. The same is true of Manon's solos, such as her aria in the second act, 'In quelle trine morbide' ('In those golden hangings'), which she sings in response to her brother's compliments, hinting at her growing dissatisfaction with her comfortable but empty life. Her duet with Des Grieux, 'Tu, tu, amore?' ('Is it you, you my love?'), which they sing when he comes to her at Geronte's house, is better known but her final solo, 'Sola, perduta, abbandanata' ('Alone, lost, abandoned'), which she sings when Des Grieux has gone off, trying to find water or shelter, has never achieved the popularity of the great soprano arias in Puccini's later operas.

In the earlier acts there are some good ensembles and there is a clever use of themes, particularly in the Le Havre scene, when Manon talks to Des Grieux through the barred window of the barracks. Lescaut has no full aria but he has some pleasing solos and the role is an important one. The short final act may seem something of an anticlimax and Manon's death hasn't quite the pathos of those of some of Puccini's later heroines, perhaps because of a feeling that she has brought some of her troubles onto herself.

This may be the result of the missing episode which is only hinted at in her final aria. She tells us that until her 'fatal beauty' attracted another admirer, America seemed a 'peaceful' country, so we can assume that she and Des Grieux were living happily together and she was being faithful to him. If the incident that brought them to their final plight had been shown it might have been seen more clearly as a misfortune that was in no way her fault and she would have come nearer to being Puccini's heroine who 'cannot fail to win the hearts of the public'.

With more time, Illica and Giacosa might have remedied the structural faults in the opera and made the final act more coherent, but it's probably fair to say that there must have been quite a lot of the work of Oliva and Praga that they felt good enough to keep in the finished opera. It may even be that if Puccini had not alienated the two men with his constant changes of mind, their original libretto might have been used and shown to be completely satisfactory.

If that had happened, however, Illica and Giacosa would not have come together to collaborate with Puccini, and their importance in his future career cannot be overstressed. *Manon Lescaut* helped Puccini to overcome the setback of *Edgar* and put him firmly back on the way to success. It was probably the quality of his music that made the structural faults seem unimportant, so that success was probably assured – but without the contribution of Illica and Giacosa, his next three operas might not have been quite the glittering triumphs that they were.

5

La Bohème

Libretto by Giuseppe Giacosa and Luigi Illica
Based on *Scènes de la Vie de Bohème* by Henri Murger

Premiere – Teatro Regio, Turin, 1 February 1896
Conductor – Arturo Toscanini

CAST

Rodolfo, a poet	Tenor	Evan Gorga
Mimi, a seamstress	Soprano	Cesira Ferrani
Marcello, a painter	Baritone	Tieste Wilmant
Musetta, a singer	Soprano	Camilla Pasini
Schaunard, a musician	Baritone	Antonio Pini-Corsi
Colline, a philosopher	Bass	Michele Mazzara
Benoît, their landlord	Bass	Alessandro Polonini
Alcindoro, a state councillor	Bass	Alessandro Polonini
Parpignol, a toy vendor	Tenor	Dante Zucchi
A customs sergeant	Bass	Felici Fogli

In March 1893, not long after he had had his first major success with *Manon Lescaut*, Puccini met the composer Leoncavallo in a coffee shop in Milan and they began to discuss their current projects. Quite casually, Puccini mentioned that he was working on an operatic version of *Scènes de la Vie de Bohème* – stories based on his days as a struggling writer in Paris by the French novelist Henry Murger.

Leoncavallo immediately became very angry and reminded Puccini that only few months earlier he had offered him a libretto that he had written on the same theme. He said that he was now composing his own score for the opera and that his offer should have warned Puccini of his interest.

We don't know how Puccini responded to this, but the following day Leoncavallo made an announcement in the newspaper *Il Secolo* (*The Sentry*), which was owned by his publisher. He said that he had been working on *La Bohème* for some time and consequently he thought that Puccini should defer to him. Puccini immediately responded by writing to another newspaper. He said that he had acted in good faith in the matter of *La Bohème* and if Leoncavallo had made it clear that he intended to compose the opera, then of course he would never have considered it. However, having now spent two months working on it, he could not now oblige 'Maestro Leoncavallo' by abandoning it. He could not see why it should matter to Leoncavallo – 'Let him compose and I shall compose, and the public will judge.'

Puccini's claim to have spent the previous two months working on *La Bohème* would have been as hard to justify as his denial that he had known of Leoncavallo's interest. Leoncavallo would hardly have claimed to have offered him the libretto if that had not been true, and it was known that following the successful premiere of *Manon Lescaut* Puccini had told several of his friends that he was planning to compose an opera based on 'La Lupa' ('The She-Wolf'), a short story by the Sicilian author Giovanni Verga. It seems, therefore, that he was being less than honest about the whole episode.

The truth was probably that when Leoncavallo offered him the libretto, *Manon Lescaut* was in the final stages of completion or nearing the rehearsal stage, so Puccini would not have had much time to think about future projects. He would not in any case have wanted to work again with Leoncavallo, having been unimpressed with his work during their brief collaboration on *Manon Lescaut*, so he would not have taken him up on his offer. At the same time, however, he probably realised that the Murger stories had good possibilities for an opera. Meeting Leoncavallo again in Milan might well have reminded him of the earlier approach so his casual remark that he was working on *La Bohème* could have been a way of establishing a claim to the story.

Unfortunately for Leoncavallo, he had no legal claim to *La Bohème* – Murger had died without heirs some years earlier – so, as Puccini had suggested, both men began to compose. Ricordi engaged Giacosa and Illica as the librettists and although there were times when he had to smooth over disagreements between the three men, *La Bohème* was completed unusually quickly for a Puccini opera. It was premiered in February 1896 – a little less than three years after the meeting with Leoncavallo that probably decided him upon the production. It was all the more remarkable because in 1894, he again started to think about 'La Lupa' and actually went to Sicily to discuss the idea with Verga. It's believed that he finally decided against it when he discussed the story with a female acquaintance whom he met on the journey home and she convinced him that it was unsuitable for an opera.

Puccini's *La Bohème* was first performed a year before Leoncavallo's opera had its premiere and at the time Leoncavallo's version was given a better reception by the critics. That may have been because it was felt that Puccini had been unethical in going ahead with the opera and dishonest in his justification of it because Leoncavallo's *Bohème* never caught on with audiences and is now rarely performed. By contrast, Puccini's version was, deservedly, an instant success and its popularity has never waned.

La Bohème opens on Christmas Eve in the garret in Paris where Rodolfo the poet – based on Murger – lives with his friends, Marcello the painter, Schaunard the musician, and Colline the philosopher. They are the Bohemians. The opening theme is a lively one that Puccini adapted from his *Capriccio Sinfonico*, which had been his 'finishing exercise' when he completed his studies at the Milan Conservatorium. It's used throughout the opera when the

Bohemians are together although in the opening scene Schaunard and Colline are absent. Rodolfo is trying to complete a magazine article and Marcello is at his easel, working on a painting of the Israelites crossing the Red Sea.

Rodolfo looks out of the window and sings of the smoke rising from the chimneys – 'Nei cieli bigi' ('In the grey skies, I see Paris smoking from a thousand chimney tops'). The room is bitterly cold and the two men consider breaking their last remaining chair for firewood but then Rodolfo offers the manuscript of the first act of a play that he has written – referring to it ironically as 'his fiery drama' and they burn that instead. Colline enters, cold and dispirited because he went out to try to sell some old books, only to find that the pawnshops were closed on Christmas Eve. The second act of Rodolfo's play goes onto the fire, quickly followed by the third, but the paper burns down too quickly to give any real heat and Marcello and Colline call, 'Abasso l'autor' – ('Down with the author') – then Schaunard comes in and the mood lightens.

Schaunard has brought food and wine and some firewood. He has just completed an unusual but well-paid engagement for an eccentric English aristocrat who hired him to play to drown the sound of parrot dying in the next apartment. He tells his friends that he finally bribed a maid to feed the bird with parsley to choke it.

The Bohemians are about to fall on the food and wine that Schaunard has brought, but their landlord Benoît appears, making one of his frequent, unsuccessful attempts to collect the rent that they owe him. There is no money to pay him but Rodolfo and Marcello trick him. They have heard that he has been seen with a young girl and they offer him wine, then encourage him to talk about his affair. As they hoped, he is more than happy to boast about his conquest, whereupon they pretend to be shocked at his behaviour and throw him out.

Rodolfo, Marcello and Colline are about to return to the food and wine but Schaunard says that it can be kept for another occasion and they should go out to celebrate Christmas Eve. They decide to go out to one of their favourite haunts, the Café Momus, but Rodolfo says that he will join them later, when he has finished his article. The others go out and Rodolfo sits down at the table to continue his work. What follows is one of the most magical operatic scenes ever written.

There is a knock at the door and Rodolfo opens it to find a young woman outside. This is Mimi, who has just come to live in the building. She says that her candle has blown out on the stairs and asks Rodolfo for a match to relight it. Rodolfo invites her in. Mimi coughs as he enters – she is consumptive – then faints and Rodolfo gives her some wine to revive her. He lights her candle for her but as she goes to the door she finds that she has dropped the key to her own apartment. The candle blows out again as the door opens and Rodolfo, anxious to keep her there, craftily blows his own one out. They begin to search for the key by the light of the moon which is shining into the room.

Rodolfo touches Mimi's hand and remarks on how cold it is. This is sung in the aria, one of the best known of Puccini's, 'Che gelida manina' ('Such a cold little hand'). He tells her about himself and how he almost makes a living as a poet, then asks her to tell him her own story. Mimi responds with the aria, another great favourite, 'Si, mi chiamano Mimi' ('Yes, they call me Mimi'). There is a slight interruption as Rodolfo's friends call from outside, urging him to hurry, and he tells them to go on to the café and reserve two places. He turns to see Mimi standing in the moonlight and the act ends with the great love duet, 'O soave fanciulla, o dolce viso di mite circonfuso alba luna' ('Oh lovely maiden, your sweet face bathed in the light of the moon'). The final lines are usually sung from outside the room as they go off together, already in love, to join Rodolfo's friends.

Puccini couldn't have known that 'Che gelida manina', 'Si, mi chiamano Mimi' and 'O soave fanciulla' would become some of the greatest favourites of operatic and concert audiences. Had he done so, he might well have wondered if the rest of *La Bohème* would be an anticlimax after they had all been performed, one after another, at the end of the first act. It isn't, however, and probably for the same reason that a story apparently so simple makes such a compelling opera. Even the most carping of operatic critics have admitted that although 'O soave fanciulla' is sentimental in the extreme, it's so good of its kind that that doesn't matter, and this is why it succeeds. Puccini followed his inspiration and 'went for broke' – and he succeeded brilliantly.

Act 2 takes place by the Café Momus, opening with a crowd scene with an air of festivity for Christmas Eve. In among the sounds of street vendors and people milling around them we hear Schaunard buying a horn and Colline haggling over a coat, while Marcello moves about in the crowd. Rodolfo takes Mimi into a milliner's shop and buys her a new bonnet, then introduces her to his friends. Eventually, they all sit down together outside the café and order a meal. A toy-seller, Parpignol, comes through the crowd with children flocking around him. There are short solos, very similar in tune by Rodolfo and Mimi, but the highpoint of the act is an aria sung by Musetta, Marcello's former lover, who appears on the scene when Parpignol has gone on his way.

Musetta is with her latest admirer Alcindoro, an elderly Councillor of State. Seeing Marcello there, she sets out to attract him with what is sometimes called Musetta's Waltz Song, the aria 'Quando me'n vo' soletta per la via' ('As I walk along through the streets'). This is a beautiful, haunting melody, once used as a popular song, 'One Night of Love'. Marcello does his best to ignore Musetta but later, when she sends Alcindoro off to have her shoe mended, he joins her and the others in a rousing sextet, after which he and Musetta sing 'Quando me'n vo' together.

Marcello and Musetta are reunited – for a while at least, as their relationship is always a volatile one. The Bohemians find that Schaunard's money isn't enough to pay the bill but Musetta manages to have it charged to Alcindoro. They exit quickly and the act ends with Alcindoro returning with Musetta's shoe and being horrified to find the very large bill in his name.

Act 3 takes place some weeks later, at dawn on a cold February morning, by a toll gate at the Barrière d'Enfer, a gate leading out of Paris by the road towards Orléans. Nearby is a tavern called The Port of Marseilles, with Marcello's Red Sea painting changed to be used as its sign. Sounds of music and laughter can be heard from inside, while outside, with snow on the ground, some customs guards sit round a brazier. The act opens in a quiet, atmospheric way, with the stage almost in darkness. The festivity of Christmas is over and it is the bleakest part of winter. As we learn, this reflects the relationship of Rodolfo and Mimi, which has changed dramatically after its romantic beginning. Even the sounds of revelry from the tavern are muted and harps and flutes suggest falling snow.

One of the customs guards opens the gate to let in some street sweepers and peasants with their carts and Musetta's voice is heard, singing the beginning of 'Quando me'n vo'', in a slower, sombre version. Puccini then begins the real action of the act with two chords in quick succession and, to the theme of 'Si, me chiamano Mimi', Mimi enters. She is coughing but manages to ask one of the customs officers if he knows of a tavern where an artist is working. He sends her to The Port of Marseilles, where Marcello has been adapting his painting for the inn sign and painting pictures for the walls. He and Musetta, still together, have been living there for the last month.

When he comes out, Mimi tells him that her life with Rodolfo has been difficult and that he has now left her – 'O buon Marcello aiuto!' ('Oh good Marcello, help me'). Rodolfo has actually been asleep inside the inn but he comes out, looking for Marcello. Mimi hides from him and when the two men talk she overhears him telling Marcello that he left her because of her flirtatious ways, but then he admits that the real reason was that she is suffering from consumption and, living in poverty as he is, he cannot help her. He hopes that his pretended jealousy will make her look for a more wealthy companion – 'Marcello, finalmente' ('Marcello, finally'). Knowing that Mimi is listening to them, Marcello tries to stop him from saying more but she has already heard what he has said.

Rodolfo then hears her coughing and when she emerges from her hiding place, they sing together of their former love.

They decide to part and Mimi sings 'Donde lieta uscì' ('Back to the home she left at her lover's voice sad Mimi must return, heavy-hearted'), her recognition that their affair is over. At the end of the aria she and Rodolfo sing together – 'Addio senza rancor' ('Goodbye without bitterness'). While they are talking Marcello and Musetta begin one of their fiery quarrels and the duet becomes a quartet – 'Addio dolce svegliare alla mattina!' ('Goodbye, sweet awakening in the morning!'). They part angrily but Rodolfo and Mimi realise that they still love each other and as a compromise they agree to remain together until the winter is over – in the spring, they won't feel so cold sleeping alone.

Puccini ends the scene, and the act, as he began it with the two chords in quick succession, which is a masterful touch. Until the chords are repeated at the end of the act most of the audience, especially those seeing the opera for the first time, will probably have forgotten them, but instantly remember them when they are repeated. It's as though Puccini, having called attention at the beginning, has made his point but gives it a final emphasis.

Act 4 of *La Bohème* begins like Act 1, with Rodolfo and Marcello in the garret trying to work. The orchestra plays the 'Bohemian' theme which opened the first act, then goes into the tune of 'Che gelida manina', heralding some nostalgia. As in the opening scene, the two men stop working, but this time to regret their lost loves in the duet 'O Mimi, tu più non torni' ('Oh Mimi, you will never return'). They have heard that Mimi and Musetta have been seen with new admirers.

Colline and Schaunard arrive and there is some attempt at jollity, but then Musetta comes in to announce that Mimi has left her new lover and is outside, seriously ill. She believes she is dying and wishes to be with Rodolfo for her remaining hours. When she comes in she is helped onto the couch and because her hands are cold she asks for a muff. Musetta gives her earrings to Marcello so that he can sell them and use the money to buy medicine. Colline gives Mimi his old coat to use as a blanket and sings a short aria, 'Vecchia zimarra' ('My old coat'). This is known as 'The Coat Song' and, although it's a bass aria, the great tenor Caruso once felt moved to record it.

The rest of the act is a tear-jerker but a good one. Puccini repeats the themes of happier days to good effect. When they are left alone Mimi begins a duet with Rodolfo, 'Sono andati?' ('Have they gone?'), and later she tries to sing 'Che gelida manina', which is continued by the orchestra when the effort is too much for her. She dies shortly afterwards, when the others have returned from their various errands. Rodolfo is unaware of it as he is draping Musetta's cloak over the window to keep out the sun. Schaunard is the first to realise it, then the silence of the others tells Rodolfo what has happened.

With its very fine score and, due to Puccini's handling of it, compelling story, it was unsurprising that *La Bohème* was given an enthusiastic reception at the premiere. With the exception of the Turin *Fanfulla*, however, press reviews were at best cool and, in most cases, hostile. One critic suggested that Puccini had composed the score 'hurriedly' – perhaps inferring that he had been anxious to complete his version of the opera before Leoncavallo's was staged. This was amusing as Puccini had offended Illica during the production stage with his comments – which, he said in a letter to Ricordi, he had made to ensure 'that the work should be what it ought to be: logical, terse and well balanced'. Had he been concerned only with finishing the opera quickly, Puccini would hardly have caused a rift with his librettist over the quality of the piece and, in doing so, delayed its completion. The same critic also predicted that the opera 'will leave no great trace on the history of our lyric theatre' – which suggests that, as far as critics are concerned, nothing very much has changed over the years.

The success of *La Bohème* was quickly assured and it's now probably the world's best-known opera, and certainly the most popular. It's interesting, therefore, that of all the singers who created those now famous roles at the premier, only the baritone Antonio

Pino-Corsi, who sang Schaunard, had anything like a successful career. It was necessary for Puccini to lower the whole part of Rodolfo for the tenor Evan Gorga who, Puccini said in a letter to Elvira, 'hasn't got such a bad voice but I doubt whether he will last'. In that, he was proved to be correct. Even Cesira Ferrani, the soprano who sang Mimi and three years earlier had created the role of Manon Lescaut, retired from the operatic stage at the early age of thirty-seven and is now virtually forgotten, as are Gorga, Tieste Wilmant (who was Marcello), Camilla Pasini (Musetta) and Michele Mazzara (the original Colline).

One person involved in the premiere of *La Bohème* who did go on to have a successful musical career was the conductor, the great Arturo Toscanini. It was Puccini's first association with him. He was actually Recordi's choice as conductor – Puccini had suggested the very able Leopoldo Mugnone but the premiere was at the Teatro Regio in Turin where Toscanini, then twenty-eight, had just been appointed as its Musical Director. It was probably for that reason that Ricordi engaged him and Puccini, quickly recognising his talents, gratefully acknowledged the wisdom of Ricordi's decision.

During his career, Toscanini conducted many performances of Puccini's operas, which is one of the most valid arguments against critics who often deride his works as shallow and 'saccharine'. Toscanini was one of the outstanding musicians of his day, partly because he was one of the greatest perfectionists. He would hardly have been associated with the operas if, as some experts have said, they were a 'box of tricks', albeit a very good one. Working and rehearsing with Puccini many times, he would have recognised a sincerity in his approach that many of his critics have failed to notice. This is often apparent in his touching belief in some of his characters.

When he wrote to Elvira about the rehearsals of *La Bohème* he expressed concern over Wilmant's portrayal of Marcello, which he thought to be somewhat coarse, adding, 'And he *is* such a gentle man.' It was probably more than a composer's figure of speech – he thought of Marcello as a real person. Many years after the opera was first produced he told his biographer Arnaldo Fraccaroli that when he had written Mimi's death scene, 'I began to weep like a child. It was as though I had seen my own child die.'

As a man and a composer, Puccini has always had his critics, but a better side of his character was revealed through his music. His other interests were mundane and he never displayed any great powers of intellect, philosophy or idealism. He made few friends and in most of his affairs with women the relationships were probably no more than physical. It is, however, a different Puccini who emerges from his correspondence with Ricordi, Elvira and Sybil Seligman when his operas were being created or when he was helping to supervise the productions of them.

He was critical in a way that revealed an understanding of his subject that was vast and clearly inborn; he was demanding of collaborators and performers, and stern in his judgements. Except in one or two personal disputes, which even at the time he probably regretted, his comments come down to us in a calm, almost resigned way as if he felt the standards he required would never be quite attained. In spite of this, his music could be as deeply emotional as the feeling for it that he revealed to Fraccaroli, and its lasting appeal owes much to a brilliant combination of professionalism and inspiration.

There is no better example of this than *La Bohème*. In lesser hands it could be seen as nothing more than an over-sentimental sob story, but Puccini made it musically enchanting, theatrically convincing and consequently a work of deserved and enduring popularity. However many times we may see it, the spell never fails to work.

6

Tosca

Libretto by Giuseppe Giacosa and Luigi Illica
Based on *La Tosca* by Victorien Sardou

Premiere – Teatro Costanzi, Rome, 14 January 1900
Conductor – Leopoldo Mugnone

CAST

Floria Tosca, a famous singer	Soprano	Hariclea Darclée
Mario Cavaradossi, an artist	Tenor	Emilio de Marchi
Scarpia, Chief of Police	Baritone	Eugenio Giraldoni
Angelotti, escaped prisoner	Bass	Ruggero Galli
Sacristan	Bass	Ettore Borelli
Spoletta, a police agent	Tenor	Enrico Giordano
Sciarrone, a gendarme	Bass	Giuseppe Gironi
Gaoler	Bass	Aristide Parassani
Shepherd Boy	Alto	Angelo Righi

La Tosca, the most successful play by the French dramatist Victorien Sardou, was premiered in Paris on 24 November 1887 with the legendary Sarah Bernhardt in the title role. When it was performed in Italy, Puccini saw it twice, in Milan and Turin, and in May 1889 he wrote to his publisher, Giulio Ricordi, urging him to obtain Saudou's permission to base an opera on it. It was not, however, until August 1895 that Puccini finally signed a contract to compose the work.

There are various versions of how the opera finally came to Puccini. It's known that, initially, Sardou said that he would rather a French composer adapted the play. Even when he had reached an agreement with Ricordi, he was reluctant that the task should be given to Puccini as he did not like his music and regarded him as unproven. Offended, Puccini declined to continue with the project and Ricordi commissioned another composer, Alberto Franchetti. Luigi Illica began writing the libretto but Franchetti never felt confident with the assignment and when Puccini renewed his interest in it, Ricordi somehow managed to persuade him to withdraw. According to one account, he convinced Franchetti that the story was too violent to succeed as an opera but it has also been reported that it was Illica who used that argument. Franchetti's family often claimed that he had nobly stepped aside because he thought that Puccini would make a better job of the opera as 'He has more time than I do.'

Whatever the reason, Puccini began work on the opera with Giacosa and Illica, who had so fortunately come together during the production of *Manon Lescaut* and continued with him to write the libretto for *La Bohème*. Even with two successful operas behind them there were difficulties and it was nearly five years later when *Tosca* was finally performed. There were, as ever, heated disagreements between the three men and Puccini was shocked when Ricordi severely criticised some duets that he had composed for the third act. They were not changed, however, and when it was finally premiered, the opera was well received by the audience. It has remained one of Puccini's must popular works.

Tosca is set in Rome, in June 1800, in three locations which still exist today. Napoleon had entered Rome and set up a republic but his army has withdrawn from the city and it has been occupied by troops of the Kingdom of Naples. Officials of the former Roman Republic have been imprisoned, but with Napoleon's troops invading the north of Italy the rule of Naples is in danger. Anyone with republican sympathies is regarded with suspicion by the Chief of Police, Baron Scarpia, a corrupt and unscrupulous Sicilian.

There is no overture and the curtain rises to three sinister rasping chords, which are the theme for Scarpia, whose malevolent presence dominates the opera. The action begins in the church of Sant'Andrea della Valle, where the artist Mario Cavaradossi is painting a picture of Mary Magdalene. Cavaradossi is absent when Cesare Angelotti, a former Consul of the Roman Republic, comes thankfully into the church. He has escaped from prison with the help of his sister, the Marchesa Attavanti, who has left some food and the key of the Attavantis' private chapel in the church, in a basket at the feet of an image of the Virgin. Hearing footsteps approaching, Angelotti takes the key and hides in the chapel. The sacristan of the church enters and, as he is reciting the Angelus, Cavaradossi appears.

Cavaradossi studies his painting and the sacristan notices that the face is that of a fair-haired, blue-eyed woman – actually the Marchesa Attavanti – who comes to the church to pray. He disapproves of using the face of a 'frivolous woman' in a religious painting but Cavaradossi muses over the 'strange harmony of contrasts, deliciously blending' between the blonde woman and his dark-haired, dark-eyed lover, Floria Tosca. This is the popular tenor aria 'Recondita armonia'.

The sacristan goes off, still muttering his disapproval, and Angelotti emerges from the chapel. Cavaradossi instantly recognises him and, as a supporter of the former republic, agrees to help him evade Scarpia, who Angelotti says is pursuing him. As they talk, Tosca arrives in the church and calls to Cavaradossi, who does not answer her until Angelotti has once again hidden in the chapel. Hearing their whispered voices, Tosca, who is extremely jealous, suspects that he was talking to another woman. Cavaradossi reassures her and she sings that she is looking forward to a night of love together – 'Non la sospiri, la nostra casetta?' ('Do you not long for our little house?') – but she then becomes jealous again when she recognises the woman in the painting as the Marchesa Attavanti, commenting on her blue eyes. Cavaradossi says that he must have seen the Marchesa at prayer and, without realising it, used her face for the painting. He and Tosca sing the duet 'Qual' occhio al mondo' ('Which eyes in the world could compare with yours?'). Tosca is finally placated and she leaves, but with a last instruction to Cavaradossi to make the eyes in his painting brown – like her own.

When she has gone, Angelotti reappears and a canon is heard in the distance, signalling that his escape has been discovered. He tells Cavaradossi that he intends to leave disguised as a woman, using some clothes that his sister has left in the chapel. He and Cavaradossi then leave for the artist's villa, where there is a hiding place in the well in the garden. When they have gone, the sacristan comes in with some choirboys who are to sing a Te Deum. They are excited because of news that Napoleon has been defeated at the Battle of Marengo, but their celebrations are suddenly stopped by the arrival of Scarpia, who is searching for Angelotti. The Scarpia theme is heard as he strides purposefully in, contrasting savagely with the merry singing of the choirboys and the sacristan.

Scarpia questions the sacristan and learns that Cavaradossi is painting the picture in the church. He then finds a fan with the Atavanti crest on it. Knowing that the Marchesa is Angelotti's sister, he is convinced that he has been in the church and that Cavaradossi, whom he suspects of being a subversive, was involved in his escape. Scarpia is a womaniser and he would like to include Tosca among his conquests. He knows that Cavaradossi is her lover and when Tosca returns to the church he begins to play on her well-known jealousy by showing her the fan that he has found. Convinced that Cavaradossi has been meeting the Marchesa there, she is furious and she rushes off to accuse him.

Scarpia muses that his agents will follow her and she will lead them to wherever Cavaradossi has hidden Angelotti. If he can recapture Angelotti and convict Cavaradossi, it will leave the way clear for him to further his pursuit of Tosca. As Scarpia imagines his triumph, the choir can be heard in the background, beginning the Te Deum, and as they parade into the church he is finally reminded of the religious occasion and sings with them. The act closes with the Scarpia theme being repeated and varied several times. It's an impressive and atmospheric finale to the act, suggesting the impending evil in Scarpia's plans.

The second act is set in Scarpia's apartment in the Farnese Palace. Scarpia, who is taking his supper, is still musing over his plans – which are sadistic. In his aria 'Ha più forte sapore' ('For myself, the violent conquest') he explains that he does not like the easy seduction, preferring one that is hard-won – and by inference, causing anguish. He intends to hang Cavaradossi if he can prove him guilty of helping Angelotti and to inflict himself on Tosca. He sends a note to Tosca, asking her to join him.

Scarpia's chief agent Spoletta comes in and admits that he has failed to find Angelotti. This angers Scarpia but he is placated when Spoletta tells him that he has arrested Cavaradossi, as he suspects that he was hiding Angelotti. Cavaradossi is brought in and questioned while, offstage, Tosca is heard singing a cantata in celebration of Napoleon's defeat at Marengo. Tosca comes to the chamber and Cavaradossi, who has denied all knowledge of Angelotti's whereabouts, is removed to an adjoining room to be tortured. Before he is taken out he manages to tell Tosca to remain silent.

As Cavaradossi is tortured and his screams of pain are heard, Scarpia presses Tosca, telling her that she can spare her lover more pain by revealing Angelotti's hiding place. At first she resists but finally gives in as more cries from Cavaradossi are heard. He is brought back into the room unconscious; when he is revived, he is furious with Tosca when he is told of her betrayal. News then arrives that Napoleon has finally won the Battle of Marengo and Cavaradossi triumphantly shouts, 'Vittoria! Vittoria!' ('Victory! Victory!') before he is led away and Tosca is left alone with Scarpia.

Knowing that she is now vulnerable, Scarpia tries to further his conquest of Tosca, and he is quite blatant about his methods – 'Già, mi dicon venal' ('Yes, they say that I am venal'). He will take advantage of his position to gain whatever he wants. He then makes Tosca an offer – if she will submit to him, he will free Cavaradossi. Tosca is horrified his at his proposal and expresses her dismay in the aria 'Vissi d'arte,

Vissi d'amore' ('I lived for art, I lived for love, never did I harm a living creature … why, O Lord, why am I repaid in this way?').

As Scarpia waits impassively for her answer, Spoletta comes in and reports that Angelotti committed suicide when they tried to arrest him. Finally Tosca agrees and Scarpia he tells her that he will arrange for Cavaradossi to face a fake execution by firing squad, after which the lovers can escape from the country. He calls Spoletta and tells him to arrange for the execution to be carried out like that of a previous prisoner, Count Palmieri. Spoletta goes out, pointedly repeating the instruction – 'Come Palmieri' ('Like Palmieri').

Scarpia writes out a safe passage for Tosca and Cavaradossi and when he has signed it he reaches out to take her. Tosca, however, has seen a knife on the supper table and, taking it up, she stabs him with it. As he dies she taunts him – 'This is how Tosca kisses' – but when he finally lies dead on the floor, she arranges candles around him and places a crucifix on his body. This is done in silence, finally broken when she sings in a low but triumphant voice, 'E avanti a lui tremava tutta Roma!' ('And before him all Rome trembled'). The respected critic and musicologist Ernest Newman (1868–1959) described this as 'the most impressively macabre scene in all opera'. The act then ends with Tosca, having taken the safe passage from Scarpia's hand, stealing quietly out of the room.

The third act takes place at the Castel Sant'Angelo, where Cavaradossi is being held. It begins with a short passage played by the horns then, because it's early in the morning, the bells for matins begin to ring. From offstage a shepherd boy is heard singing 'Io de' sospiri' ('I give you sighs'). The gaoler tells Cavaradossi that he will be executed in an hour and in the aria 'E lucevan le stelle' ('And the stars shone brightly') he recalls his nights of love with Tosca. The aria ends on a note of despair but the mood suddenly brightens as Tosca appears. Excitedly, she tells him the bargain Scarpia tried to make with her and then 'a knife gleamed and with that knife I stabbed him!' She seems overawed by her deed but gives the impression that, faced with that situation again, she would do exactly the same.

A series of duets follow: 'O dolci mani' ('Oh sweet hands, pure and gentle') as Cavaradossi sympathises with Tosca that her hands were stained with Scarpia's blood, and then, to music that was cut from the later versions of *Edgar*, he assures her that he only felt 'the sting of death' for her – 'Amaro sol per te m'era il morire!' They picture their life together when they have escaped and left the country and there is a short, exultant passage which they sing in unison with the orchestra silent, to the theme played by the horns at the start of the act. As the duet ends and the orchestra plays again, Tosca sings quietly and tenderly, 'Gli occhi ti chiudero con mille bacchii e mille ti daro nomi d'amore' ('I shall close your eyes with a thousand kisses and call you a thousand loving names').

In opera moments of supreme happiness seldom last and critics have commented that Spoletta's studied repetition of Scarpia's instruction 'Come Palmieri' should have warned Tosca that all would not be as Scarpia promised. It's often sensed by those members of the audience who have not seen the opera before. The lovers' moment of joy is ended by the arrival of the firing squad and it's time for the fake execution to be enacted. Tosca urges Cavaradossi to play his part properly and when he is led away she is impatient at how long the final ceremonies are taking. At last, a volley of shots ring out and Tosca enthuses at how well Cavaradossi has pretended to fall dead – 'Ecco un artista!' ('What an actor!'). The soldiers march out and Tosca runs to Cavaradossi urging him to get up so that they can escape – but then she realises that Scarpia has tricked her and he really is dead.

As she weeps hysterically over the body, voices are heard and Spoletta and his men rush in. He has found Scarpia's body and, realising that it was Tosca who killed him, he has come to arrest her. Tosca evades him and runs to the battlements. Then, with a final cry to Scarpia that they will meet again before God ('Avanti a Deo') she leaps to her death. The opera ends with the orchestra playing the final passage of Cavaradossi's aria 'E lucevan le stelle'.

Puccini had wanted Toscanini to conduct at the premiere but Ricordi had arranged for it to be staged in Rome, at the Teatro

Costanzi, and Toscanini was engaged at La Scala, Milan. Leopoldo Mugnone, whom Puccini had actually wanted to conduct the premiere of *La Bohème*, was engaged. It began as a slightly bizarre occasion, mainly because it was staged at a time of political and social unrest. The police had received warnings that anarchists might bomb the theatre and the premiere was postponed by one day to 14 January 1900. As the time to raise the curtain approached, the police were still worried about possible disturbances and told Mugnone that if there was any sign of trouble he was to lead the orchestra into the national anthem.

The performance was well attended, as a Puccini premiere was already an important theatrical event. Other operatic composers were present as well as the prime minister and several members of his cabinet. The opera began on time but very soon stopped when people began to enter the auditorium and there was a call to lower the curtain. It was actually latecomers so Mugnone was soon able to start again and the performance was completed without any more interruptions.

The critics were generally less enthusiastic than the audience, and although *Tosca* soon became a favourite with opera-goers, critical opinion has remained divided. Some have criticised the adaptation of Sardou's play, and the British composer Benjamin Britten complained of 'the cheapness and emptiness of Puccini's music'. The Australian expert Charles Osborne, however, has attributed the continuing popularity of the opera to 'the taut effectiveness of its melodramatic plot, the opportunities given to its three leading characters to shine vocally and dramatically, and the presence of two great arias, "Recondita armonia" and "E lucevan le stelle"'.

A persistent critic of Puccini has been the American musicologist Joseph Kerman, who, until his retirement in 1994, held posts at various universities. He described *Tosca* as 'a shabby little shocker' – which was hardly original as it was well known that George Bernard Shaw's comment on Sardou's play had been, 'What a tawdry little shocker, if only it were an opera.' The opera ends with the theme from Cavaradossi's aria, 'E lucevan le stelle', and Kerman jibed that 'the orchestra screams the first thing that comes into its head'.

More objective critics have pointed out that the phrase played accompanies the line, 'My dream of love is ended', which, as Cavaradossi and his lover are both dead, is quite a fair summing up of the situation. Kerman might have been more accurate if he had said that the orchestra plays the first thing that came into Puccini's head, which was likely because he was nothing if not inspirational.

Some musical experts have, in fact, attributed Puccini's success to his 'theatrical flair' rather than his music – which contradicts the opinions of others who have said that he was never a great theatrical composer – but this ignores his professionalism and attention to detail. He went to the Castel Sant'Angelo to gauge the sound of the matins bells as they would be heard from there at the start of the third act, and he had bells cast to order by four different foundries to reproduce the authentic sound. When he wrote the music for the Te Deum procession at the end of the first act, he adapted it to the exact pitch of the great bell of St Peter's basilica. He also showed a touch of sentimentality by including in the background music in the second act an adaptation of a student exercise which written fifteen years earlier by his late brother Michele. He thought that by its inclusion in his opera, his brother would live again through him.

Since 1890 Tosca has been performed countless times, in many different countries. Most of the great tenors – including Caruso, Gigli and Pavarotti – have sung the part of Cavaradossi while the incomparable Maria Callas is still widely regarded as the definitive Tosca. She often starred with the renowned baritone Tito Gobbi as Scarpia. There have also been performances in other settings, such as a production in Florence in 1986 under the British director Jonathan Miller. This transferred the action to Rome in 1944, under the German occupation.

In 1992 there was a remarkable production starring the American soprano Catherine Malfitano and Placido Domingo. It was shown live on television from the original settings – the church of Sant'Andrea della Valle, the Farnese Palace and the Castel Sant'Angelo – in three different broadcasts at the actual times that the action takes place. *The Times* referred to it as 'simply a triumph'. As the final act began at six o'clock in the morning as the dawn broke over Rome, even the most enthusiastic of us would have set our videos to record it. It was something that Puccini could never have imagined, but he would probably have enjoyed it – pleased with the performances, thrilled to see Tosca make her fatal leap with the real dome of St Peter's in the background and, as an innovator himself, fascinated by the modern technology.

7

Madama Butterfly

Libretto by Giuseppe Giacosa and Luigi Illica
Based on the short story 'Madame Butterfly' by John Luther Long

Premiere – Teatro della Scala, Milan, 17 February 1904
Conductor – Cleofonte Campanini

CAST

Madama Butterfly, Cio-Cio San	Soprano	Rosina Storchio
Suzuki, her maid	Mezzo-Soprano	Giuseppina Giaconia
Lieutenant Pinkerton, US Navy	Tenor	Giovanni Zenatello
Sharpless, US Consul	Baritone	Giuseppe de Luca
Goro, a matchmaker	Tenor	Gaetano Pini-Corsi
Prince Yamadori	Tenor	Emilio Venturini
The Bonze (Priest), Cio-Cio San's Uncle	Bass	Paolo Wulmann
Yakuside, Cio-Cio San's Uncle	Bass	Antonio Volpini
The Imperial Commissioner	Bass	Viale
The Official Registrar	Bass	Gennari
Cio-Cio San's mother	Mezzo-Soprano	Tina Alasia
The Aunt	Soprano	Ghissoni
The Cousin	Soprano	Palmira Maggi

Kate Pinkerton   Mezzo-Soprano   Manfredi

The great American jazz singer Sarah Vaughan had a favourite song, 'Poor Butterfly', which was a simplified version of the *Madama Butterfly* story. 'Poor Butterfly' ('Povera Butterfly') is actually a line from Puccini's opera *Madama Butterfly*, sung towards the end by Suzuki, the heroine's faithful maidservant and companion. The song tells of 'a little Japanese, sitting demurely 'neath the cherry trees', who sadly dies of a broken heart as she waits for her American sailor to come back to her. Anyone who had never seen Puccini's opera would probably assume that it follows the same story, but that would be very wrong.

Butterfly (Cio-Cio San) is a young Japanese girl, living in Nagasaki, and she does fall in love with an American sailor, Lieutenant Pinkerton. When the opera opens, Pinkerton and Goro, the marriage broker who has arranged the marriage, are inspecting the house where the couple will live. Sharpless, the US Consul in Nagasaki, calls and Pinkerton makes it clear to him that he is taking a very light-hearted attitude to the marriage. He says he has bought the house where they will live for 999 years but the contract has a monthly 'get out' clause and he feels that a Japanese-style marriage gives him the same right.

With Goro supervising, the wedding ceremony takes place in the house and afterwards the celebratory feast is held in the garden. The festivities are interrupted by Butterfly's uncle, the Bonze – a Buddhist priest – who curses her for renouncing her Japanese god. Although they were enjoying the celebration, the assembled relations join him in condemning her. Pinkerton angrily orders them out then, alone with Butterfly, he comforts her. At first she is uncertain and shy but gradually begins to respond to him and they go into the house together as the curtain brings the first act to its close.

The story resumes three years later with Butterfly, now with a son, waiting trustingly for Pinkerton to return. She is visited by Goro, accompanied by Sharpless, who has received a letter from Pinkerton. The Consul tells Butterfly that Pinkerton is returning, but has married his American sweetheart. The purpose of Goro's visit is to introduce a client, Prince Yamadori. He sees Butterfly as a suitable wife for the Prince and Sharpless is anxious for her to accept. Having always had misgivings about Pinkerton's attitude, he is concerned for her and he knows that if she married Yamadori she would be accepted back into Japanese society. Butterfly, however, has heard only what she wanted to hear – that Pinkerton is coming back. She receives the Prince politely but declines his offer, saying that she is already married to Pinkerton. When Sharpless tries to persuade her, she replies by showing him Pinkerton's son. She urges him to write to Pinkerton and inform him of the child's existence and, deeply moved by her words, Sharpless promises to do so.

When the Consul has gone, Butterfly and Suzuki turn on Goro, who has been spreading the story that nobody knows who is the father of Butterfly's child. He makes a hasty exit, just before the sound of a cannon is heard. Butterfly knows that this means that a ship has arrived in the harbour and, looking through a telescope that she has mounted by the window, she sees that it is the *Abraham Lincoln*, the battleship on which Pinkerton left Nagasaki. She and Suzuki gather flowers from the garden and happily decorate the house, then wait for Pinkerton to come.

Their vigil lasts throughout the night as it is only on the following morning that Pinkerton appears. When he does, he is accompanied by his American wife Kate and Sharpless, who tells Suzuki that the Pinkertons are willing to adopt the child and have come to take him. Coming back to the house after so long, Pinkerton is suddenly conscience-stricken and runs out, leaving Kate to speak to Butterfly. Suzuki manages to make her mistress understand that Pinkerton no longer regards her as his wife. Butterfly agrees to give up the child but wants Pinkerton to come to her, to take him.

When Kate and Sharpless have gone, Butterfly takes out a dagger which her father, at the Emperor's order, used to commit hara-kiri. It is inscribed, 'He dies with honour who can no longer live with honour.' Suzuki tries to deter her from taking her own life by bringing in the child but Butterfly gives him a doll to play with and an American flag to wave to greet his father, then gently blindfolds him before she goes behind a screen and stabs herself.

The story of *Madama Butterfly* was adapted from a play by the American author David Belasco, who developed it from a short story by another American, John Luther Long. Puccini saw a performance of the play in London and immediately begged Belasco to allow him to base an opera on it. It would be easy to assume that he saw Butterfly simply as his next tragic heroine but as an experienced composer, then with three successful operas behind him, he would have recognised that there was far more to her than that.

Butterfly has a tremendous strength of character which far removes her from the popular conception of the meek little Japanese girl who dies of a broken heart when she finally realises that she has been abandoned. For Pinkerton's sake she takes instruction in the Christian religion, knowing that it will alienate her from her relations and friends. Determined to remain his wife, she refuses to marry Yamadori and reinstate herself in Japanese society, but she agrees to give up her child so that he can be brought up by his natural father. Finally, when she has to accept that she will never be an American wife, she reverts to her traditional Japanese code and 'dies with honour'.

It was in the summer of 1900, a few months after the successful premiere of *Tosca*, that Puccini saw the performance of Belasco's play that so greatly attracted him to the story. In November of that year he told Ricordi that he was becoming more and more convinced that it would be the basis of a successful opera and he finally reached agreement with Belasco in April 1901. Work on the libretto began almost immediately but it was not finished until three years later. This was not a particularly long time for a Puccini opera to reach its final form, but in this case completion was not delayed only by usual changes of mind and the need to convince Illica and Giacosa of the advantages of them.

As well as music and women, Puccini had a passion for motor cars, and particularly the faster models. On a foggy night in February 1903 he sustained a broken leg when the car he was driving went off the road near Lucca. In the circumstances, he escaped lightly but the injury was badly treated and he was left with a permanent limp. The medical examination that he was given at the time also revealed that he was suffering from a mild form of diabetes. It was about four months before he could resume work and at one time he became so depressed that he told Illica that he thought it was the end of everything for him.

This was an overreaction born of frustration, but a contradictory trait of his apparently cavalier attitude to life – especially in regard to his many extramarital affairs – was that he was often prone to acute depression. In that case, when he was anxious to complete *Madama Butterfly*, the enforced inactivity would have been very difficult for him to cope with.

Although he would often take a long time to decide on the subject for a new opera and cause delays by frequently asking his librettists for alterations when he was actually composing one, he could become very impatient to complete the work when he felt that he had arrived at the exact format that he wanted. *Madama Butterfly* was at an advanced stage of production at the time of his accident and he would have been anxious to press on while everything was clear in his mind. Work on it was actually finished by the end of the year and although it left a fairly short time for rehearsals the premiere was arranged for 17 February 1904.

In those early weeks in 1904 Puccini must have felt much happier than he had a few months earlier. He had almost recovered from his accident and in January of that year he and Elvira had finally married – her husband had died in 1903. Above all, *Madama Butterfly* had been completed and was to have its premiere at La Scala, Milan – Italy's most famous opera house. *Edgar* had been premiered there in

1889 and had failed, *Manon Lescaut* and *La Bohème* had had their first performances in Turin, and *Tosca* had made its debut in Rome, where it was set. A successful premiere at La Scala was something that every operatic composer would have wanted, and when it was arranged that *Madama Butterfly* would have its first performance there, Puccini was probably pleased.

The cast was a particularly good one. Butterfly was to be sung by Rosina Storchio, whose sensitive style of singing and acting made her ideal for the part. Giovanni Zenatello, a successful Des Grieux in *Manon Lescaut*, had been given the role of Pinkerton, with the distinguished baritone Giuseppe de Luca as Sharpless. Cleofonte Campanini, the conductor, was a musician of established reputation and Giulio Ricordi's son Tito, as producer, had engaged an expert scenic designer for the stage décor. Far from ensuring success, however, all those advantages must only have made it a more crushing disappointment for Puccini when that first performance was a complete fiasco.

Boos, hisses and catcalls punctuated the performance to an extent that suggests that Puccini was probably right when he alleged afterwards that the whole thing had been orchestrated. A love duet at the end of the first act – one of Puccini's most brilliant – was subjected to catcalls and hissing and even the famous aria 'Un bel dì' ('One fine day') met with a determined silence. This was strange behaviour from a knowledgeable Italian audience. The opera was withdrawn but presented again a few weeks later at Brescia, in the north of Italy, where it was an instant success. Puccini had made some alterations but certainly not enough to explain why it had had such a different reception in Milan.

Press comment on the Milan disaster was particularly cruel, with one newspaper referring to *Butterfly* as a 'diabetic opera' and 'the result of an accident'. Would that critic have said the same if the audience had not reacted as it did? Probably not, because the notices for the very similar version performed at Brescia were far more complimentary. Campanini was again the conductor and the cast at that second performance was practically the same, so there could have been no question of the performers being at fault. The only major change at Brescia was that Rosina Storchio was replaced by the Ukrainian soprano Solomiya Krushelnytska, another singer of great acting ability. Storchio was unable to appear because she was singing the part of Butterfly in a performance in Buenos Aires. Toscanini conducted that performance, which was an endorsement of the opera as a work of art that removed any doubts raised by its reception at Milan.

Although it would not explain all the hostility shown at Milan, it could have been that the audience simply failed to appreciate the quality of the music. Puccini is often criticised for playing down to popular taste and commercial interests by peppering his operas with memorable arias and duets, but nobody could accuse him of having done so in *Madama Butterfly*. The only well-known aria is 'One fine day', which Butterfly sings in the second act when she stubbornly insists that Pinkerton will return to her. Pinkerton, the tenor lead, has no full-length aria. *Madama Butterfly* is no 'easy listening' opera but like any other worthwhile piece of music it demands something of the listener. There can be no doubts about Puccini's integrity as a composer in the way that he created it.

The opening scenes of the opera introduce all the main characters and point up what is to come. Goro, Pinkerton, Suzuki and Sharpless are all seen, and as he drinks with Sharpless before the wedding ceremony, Pinkerton reveals his cavalier attitude to the marriage in his short solo piece (introduced by a snatch of 'The Star Spangled Banner') 'Dovunque al mondo' ('Anywhere in the world') in which he tells the Consul that the 'Yankee wanderer' is not satisfied until he 'captures the flowers of every shore and the love of every beautiful woman'. He is attracted to Butterfly, as he admits in another solo, 'Amore o grille' ('Love or fancy'), but follows this by inviting Sharpness to join him in a toast to 'A real American wife', suggesting to the worried Consul that he sees her as only a temporary partner.

Butterfly is heard approaching with some friends and their entrance gives producers the opportunity to include some pretty effects with Japanese parasols. When she sees the house that Pinkerton has bought for them with its view over the harbour, she proclaims herself 'the happiest girl in Japan – all this sea, all these flowers, all this light'.

In more sombre mood she tells Sharpless how her family became impoverished, forcing her to become a geisha. She shows Pinkerton some of her personal treasures but is reticent on the subject of the inscribed dagger. Goro, who is still hovering around, mentions the orders of the Emperor and hints to Pinkerton that these included the act of hara-kiri. After the marriage ceremony Pinkerton is amused by Butterfly's relations and tells Sharpless that 'This is a farce – all these will be my new relatives for only a month.' Sharpless warns him that Butterfly is completely serious about the marriage, which is emphasised when she sings an arietta, 'Ierie son salita' ('Yesterday I went out'), in which she tells Pinkerton that she has been to the Christian mission to take instruction as she intends to convert to his faith.

There is an abrupt change of mood when her uncle, the Bonze, arrives, curses her for renouncing her religion and encourages her relations to join him in his tirade. At this point Puccini introduces a 'Curse' motif, which he uses again, later in the opera, to warn of the final tragedy. The finale of the act begins when Pinkerton, having angrily ordered the guests to go, comforts Butterfly and begins the love duet 'Viene la sera' ('Evening is falling'). It lasts for almost 15 minutes and is a beautifully written piece, moving from Pinkerton's gentle, almost embarrassed, opening words of consolation, to a serene climax as the couple go into the house together.

Earlier in the first act, at the point where Butterfly and her friends are heard approaching the house, the audience at the Milan premiere shouted 'Bohème!' – alleging that Puccini borrowed the music for their ensemble from his earlier work, but the love duet is more reminiscent of it. A phrase which is often repeated is similar to the opening line of Musetta's aria 'Quando m'en vo' but like many composers Puccini had his 'trademarks' and this in no way lessens the excellence of the duet.

As it progresses, Butterfly's mood changes as she begins to respond to Pinkerton. 'Vogliateme bene' ('Love me a little') she pleads, as if she realises that his feelings are different to her own – and she also hesitates as she recalls that Westerners sometimes impale butterflies on pins and put them in glass cases. Pinkerton reassures her, telling her he would only do that to stop her from running away from him. Butterfly then begins to surrender to her emotions, but with one more brief hesitation which makes the climax – when they are finally, if temporarily, at one with each other – all the more moving.

Puccini was probably not the greatest operatic composer that Italy ever produced, but he created some of the finest moments in the whole of opera and the end of the love duet in *Madama Butterfly* is one of them. We sense that Pinkerton will desert Butterfly but at the moment, feeling protective towards her, his affections seem genuine and this makes the duet all the more poignant. Until his later work *La Fanciulla del West*, Puccini seemed unable to present a happy and lasting love in his operas. Rodolfo and Mimi quickly fall in love and express their emotions in the great duet 'O soave fanciulla', but their happiness is short-lived. Tosca and Cavaradossi are ecstatically happy as they sing their final duets but tragedy is not far away. Butterfly, distressed by the reactions of her relations, is won over by Pinkerton but for him it's only a momentary infatuation – and we have not very long to see this.

As the curtain rises for Act 2, the 'Curse' motif is heard and Butterfly in seen in a despondent mood. Three years have passed since she last saw Pinkerton but she doggedly assures Suzuki that he will return, as he promised, 'when the robins build their nests'. Suzuki remains doubtful and, after singing a passage from the love duet, Butterfly seeks to convince her with the aria 'Un bel di'. This is a piece typical of Puccini, moving to what seems to be the climax as Butterfly imagines the scene as Pinkerton returns to her but soaring to even greater emotion as she tells Suzuki that 'with unshakeable faith' she will wait for him. Sublime though it is, there is also an unmistakeable air of desperation as she concludes the aria.

The arrival of Sharpless and Goro soon shows that Butterfly's confidence – false or otherwise – is unjustified. Sharpless tries to make her read the letter in which Pinkerton has said that he now has an American wife. Prince Yamadori, in a sedan chair, is then ushered in by Goro and is introduced with part of a Japanese tune previously used by Gilbert and Sullivan in *The Mikado*. Butterfly receives him graciously and serves tea to her visitors while the orchestra plays a slow waltz.

When Yamadori has gone, Sharpless and Butterfly take part in a duet, 'Ora a noi' ('Now to us – we'll read the letter'), in which the Consul again tries to make Butterfly understand what Pinkerton has written. He asks her what she would do if Pinkerton did not return to her and she replies that she could become a geisha again – 'that horrible trade' – or she could die, which she would prefer. When he has advised her to reconsider Yamadori's offer and she has responded by bringing in her little son, she sings the sad arietta, 'Che tua madre' ('That your mother').

The child is too young to understand her but she makes him a focus for her grief and anxiety by telling him what Sharpless has said to her. The mood becomes more animated when the Consul has gone and Butterfly and Suzuki turn on Goro and chase him out, but the sound of the ship's cannon brings about another change. Butterfly sings to a sombre reprise of 'One fine day', and from the orchestra there is the opening phrase of 'The Star Spangled Banner', and a reminder of the love duet from the first act, signifying that Pinkerton has returned but in the way that Butterfly still insists she had expected.

Butterfly gives another show of confidence as she and Suzuki decorate the house with flowers brought from the garden and sing their Flower Duet, 'Scoti quella frond di ciliego' ('Ask the cherry tree to yield its blossoms and drown my face in its flowers'). With

Butterfly's little son they then wait for Pinkerton to appear, looking out through holes which Butterfly has made in the paper walls. This is the end of the second act but there is no intermission but a humming chorus to carry the action forward. In the original version, performed at La Scala, there were only two acts but Puccini divided the second for the version put on at Brescia. The action resumes the following morning, with the two women still waiting. Butterfly sings to her child and this is where Suzuki sadly sings her line, 'Poor Butterfly'.

When Pinkerton finally arrives, he and Sharpless confer while his wife Kate waits outside. They are joined by Suzuki, who tells them 'Io so che alle sue pene' ('I know all her sorrows'). Pinkerton makes his guilt-ridden exit after the arietta 'Addio fiorito asil' ('Farewell my enchanted house, filled with blossoms and with love'). Puccini added this to the score after the Milan premiere and it has been suggested that it was because the tenor lead had very little to do in the second act except wait to come in after Butterfly has committed suicide.

Suzuki meets Kate, who, in a kindly way, asks her to tell Butterfly to trust her and says that she will be like a mother to Pinkerton's child. Butterfly enters and the 'Curse' motif is heard again. In spite of Suzuki's efforts to prevent it, she meets Kate and, finally accepting the true situation, she sings the arietta 'Sotto il gran ponte del cielo' ('Under the great arc of the sky there is no woman as lucky as you'). In the original production, this was sung by Kate but Puccini shortened her role for the revised version of the opera and gave the solo to Butterfly. It's when she has completed it that Butterfly agrees to give up her child but insists that Pinkerton must come to take him from her.

When she takes out her father's dagger and reads the inscription, Suzuki immediately realises her intention and pushes the child into the room. Butterfly sings her final farewell to him, then gives him the doll and the American flag. After blindfolding him, she goes behind the screen. Pinkerton's voice calling 'Butterfly' is heard, then he and Sharpless rush in to find her dying. Sharpless, caring as he has been throughout the opera, takes the child in his arms while the distraught Pinkerton kneels beside Butterfly.

Puccini took the title of his opera from Belasco's play but it could hardly have been called anything else. From the moment she makes her entrance in the first act until her suicide at the end, Butterfly is rarely offstage and displays the widest range of emotions. She shows girlish delight as she anticipates her marriage, distress when her uncle turns her family against her, the shyness gradually turning into ecstasy in the love duet. In the second act she gives a display of her 'unshakeable faith' as she insists that Pinkerton *will* return to her and this makes her final acceptance of the truth all the more touching. This is probably the Puccini role which calls most strongly for an accomplished actress, which is reflected by the casting of Storchio and Krushelnytska in the role.

Puccini was a composer of the 'verismo' school – a movement towards greater realism in Italian opera which had begun in the late nineteenth century – and *Madama Butterfly* is one of the best examples of it. Not only does much of the music have an authentic oriental sound but the solos and ensembles, although pleasing to hear, are mostly unspectacular and fit neatly into the action. Even the greatest arias and duets can sometimes sound contrived and therefore intrusive, but in *Madama Butterfly* there is never any hint of this. Butterfly's assertion of faith in 'One fine day' is completely valid for the moment at which she sings it and, as the only full aria in the opera, is all the more effective. The great love duet follows naturally from the action which precedes it and makes an impressive and ever more compelling finale to the first act as Pinkerton first consoles and then wins over his distressed and nervous bride.

Puccini considered *Madama Butterfly* to be his finest opera, possibly because it came nearest to achieving his aims as a verismo composer, and it has certainly received less criticism on musical and dramatic grounds than most of his works. It was unfortunate that the unjustified hostility of the audience at Milan meant that in his lifetime he was denied the pleasure of a successful premiere at La

Scala. It's possible that if he had lived to see the finished version of *Turandot*, which was completed after his death by another composer and was successfully premiered at that theatre, he might have regarded that as his greatest work. What is certain is that as an opera which succeeded and has retained its popularity with the minimum of out-and-out 'show-stoppers', *Madama Butterfly* has few if any equals.

8

La Fanciulla del West

Libretto by Guelfo Civinini and Carlo Zangarini
Based on *The Girl of the Golden West* by David Belasco

Premiere – Metropolitan House, New York, 10 December 1910
Conductor – Arturo Toscanini

CAST

Minnie	Soprano	Emmy Destinn
Jack Rance, Sheriff	Baritone	Pasquale Amato
Dick Johnson (Ramerrez)	Tenor	Enrico Caruso
Nick, a bartender	Tenor	Albert Reiss
Ashby, Wells Fargo agent	Bass	Adamo Didur
Sonora, a miner	Baritone	Dinh Gilly
Trin, a miner	Tenor	Angelo Badà
Sid, a miner	Baritone	Giulio Rossi
Handsome, a miner	Baritone	Vincenzo Reschiglian
Harry, a miner	Tenor	Pietro Audisio
Joe, a miner	Tenor	Glenn Hall
Happy, a miner	Baritone	Antonio Pini-Corsi
Jim Larkens, a miner	Bass	Bernard Bégué
Billy Jackrabbit, a Red Indian	Bass	Georges Bourgeois
Wowkle, his squaw	Mezzo-Soprano	Marie Mattfeld
Jake Wallace, a minstrel	Baritone	Andrés De Segurola

| José Castro, a 'greaser' in Ramerrez's gang | Bass | Edoardo Missiano |
| Pony Express rider | Tenor | Lamberto Belleri |

The careers of the great composers can often be divided into distinct periods and in Puccini's there were three. The first was the one in which he showed great promise with *Le Villi*, faltered with *Edgar*, but finally established himself as a major operatic composer with *Manon Lescaut*. It also saw the establishment of the successful collaboration with Illica and Giacosa. The second period was one of continuing success, with *La Bohème*, *Tosca* and *Madama Butterfly*. In a way, it came to an end with the death of Giuseppe Giacosa, after a fairly long illness in 1906, because until his final opera *Turandot*, completed two years after his death in 1924, none of his works achieved anything like the popularity of those produced with Illica and Giacosa.

Although they had many disagreements during the composing of his operas, Puccini would have recognised the value of his two librettists. When Giacosa died, he tried to find a new collaborator for Illica, who needed a writer of Giacosa's poetic ability to work with him, but when he began his next opera it was with different librettists. He remained on good terms with Illica, sometimes discussing new projects with him, but they never worked together again.

Puccini was not actually working with Giacosa when he died and it was not until July 1907, over three and a half years after the adapted version of *Madama Butterfly* had been performed at Brescia, that he actually decided upon his next production. This was not because he had departed from his usual practice of looking for a new theme as soon as one opera had been completed to his satisfaction or because there were no ideas which, as he often did, he immediately seized upon with great enthusiasm but just as suddenly rejected. As an established and popular composer, with four major operas to his name and productions of them in all the world's major centres to supervise or attend, he was often away from Italy and consequently had far less time to give any sustained thoughts to new projects.

The new opera that he decided up was based on *The Girl of the Golden West*, another play by David Belasco, whose *Madame Butterfly* had been the basis for Puccini's last opera. Under the shorter title *La Fanciulla del West (The Girl of the West)* it had its premiere at the famous Metropolitan Opera House in New York, in December 1910 – nearly seven years after *Madama Butterfly* was first staged.

Puccini saw Belasco's play in the spring of 1907 and decided that it would translate successfully into an opera when he had studied a copy of it which Sybil Seligman had obtained and had translated into Italian for him. When he began to work on it, his librettist was Carlo Zangarini, a successful dramatist who was half-American and probably seemed a good choice as the opera was to be set in the Wild West, in the days of the Californian gold rush.

Zangarini had completed two of the three acts when Puccini decided to hurry things along by bringing in another librettist, Guelfo Civinini. Whatever he may have thought about this initially, Zangarini certainly took offence when Civinini altered the first two acts. He promptly withdrew from the project, leaving Civinini to complete the third act. Whereas the changes of librettists for *Manon Lescaut* finally produced a successful and lasting collaboration for Puccini, there was no such happy outcome in this case. When he began to work on his next opera, it was with another new librettist.

La Fanciulla del West was a bold venture for Puccini. It was not the first major opera to have an unusual setting – Verdi's *Aida* was set in Ancient Egypt and his own *Madama Butterfly* was a Japanese story – but the Wild West was something else again. It would have been less daring if it had been a traditional-sounding Italian opera in an American setting; but with his verismo approach, Puccini would never have considered that option. In the same way that he was concerned to give *Madama Butterfly* authentic oriental sounds, he gave *La Fanciulla del West* a genuinely American flavour with the use of syncopated themes and authentic folk songs. It was also in accordance with the verismo style that he included only one outstanding aria which, unusually in one of his operas, was not sung by the heroine.

The 'Girl' of the title is Minnie, a strong-minded young lady who keeps a pistol in her bodice and runs the Polka Saloon in a mining camp. She also looks after the miners' gold for them and gives them Bible readings. The miners have great affection for her, as is shown in different ways throughout the opera. The local Sheriff, Jack Rance, wants to marry her, as he makes clear, and as the miners have no great liking for him, this causes resentment – especially from one named Sonora who is quietly in love with her.

The first act is set in the Polka, and opens unusually. The stage is darkened and all that can be seen is the glow of a cigar, which is being smoked by Rance, who is sitting there alone. The miners come in and Rance has to take action when one of them, Sid, is caught cheating in a card game. There is almost a fight but Rance intervenes and when he has pacified the men he pins two cards to Sid's jacket, as a sign that he is a cheat. Another man then comes to the saloon, a stranger, but it's revealed that Minnie has met him previously, on the road to the nearby town of Monterrey. He has told her that his name is Dick Johnson but he is really a notorious bandit known as Ramerrez. There was a mutual attraction between them and when he enters the saloon, obviously hoping to see her again, she makes him welcome. This angers Rance and he shows hostility and suspicion towards the stranger. Knowing their affection for Minnie, he tries to turn the assembled miners against the newcomer but, guessing his motive and resenting his intentions towards Minnie, they refuse to side with him.

As Minnie is dancing with Johnson, the Wells Fargo agent Ashby brings in Castro, a member of Ramerrez's gang, whom he has captured. Castro offers to lead a posse to the gang's hideout but when he manages to exchange words with Johnson he tells him that he has allowed himself to be captured so that he can act as a decoy. The rest of the gang are hiding nearby and plan to steal the miners' gold when Rance and the posse have left. One of them will whistle and they will come in when Johnson returns their signal. Rance goes off with the posse, leaving Minnie alone with Johnson. They talk for a while and Minnie shows Johnson where she keeps the miners' gold. She tells him that she would be killed before she would allow anyone to take it. Johnson hears the signal from his gang but he does not return it. As the act ends, the saloon is due to close and Minnie invites Johnson to come to her cabin in the mountains later that night.

The second act takes place in the cabin, where Minnie and her Indian maidservant are preparing for Johnson's visit. Minnie has dressed in her best clothes and this is so obvious that when Johnson arrives he embarrasses her by asking her if she is intending to go out. They talk and the attraction between them grows until Johnson tells Minnie that he must have a kiss from her. She agrees, reluctantly because this is all new to her and she has never before kissed a man. Outside a blizzard has begun and when Johnson says he must go, Minnie tells him that he will not be able to find the trail in the snow and insists that he should stay in the cabin for the night.

They try to sleep but there is a knock at the door and Minnie opens it to find Rance outside, accompanied by Ashby, Nick the bartender from the Polka, and Sonora, one of the miners. At her insistence, Johnson hides as they come in. They have been hunting Ramerrez, and Rance tells Minnie that he is the man who danced with her at the saloon earlier that evening. The bandit's former mistress – a local lady called Nina Micheltorena, whom Minnie regards as a 'hussy' – has given them a photograph of him which clearly identifies him as Johnson. Minnie does not tell them that Johnson is with her but Nick suspects that he is there. Johnson had bought cigars at the saloon and Nick recognises the butt of one of them in an ashtray. He does not tell Rance what he has seen, but as the others leave he offers to stay with Minnie. She thanks him but declines.

When they have all gone and they are again alone together, Johnson admits to Minnie that he is Ramerrez. He says that his present way of life was forced on him when his father died and it was revealed that he had been a bandit. Johnson had then taken over the gang as it seemed to be his only way of supporting his mother and his younger brothers, but now that he has met Minnie he would like to lead an honest life. Minnie tells him that she can forgive him for being a bandit but not for taking her first kiss under what she sees as false pretences. She asks him to leave and he goes off into the blizzard. After a few seconds Minnie hears a shot and then the sound of a body falling against the door. Johnson has been wounded and Minnie goes to his aid. She helps him to come inside, just before Rance arrives and knocks loudly on the door. With Minnie helping him, Johnson manages to climb a ladder to the loft, where he can hide from the Sheriff.

Rance searches the cabin then, thinking that Minnie is alone, he tries to kiss her. She fights him off and tells him to go but as he is about to leave, a drop of blood falls onto his hand. He realises that Johnson is in the loft and orders him to come down. Faint from the loss of blood, he manages to climb down and Minnie helps him to a chair. She then challenges Rance, a keen gambler, to play poker with her. If he wins, she will marry him and he can take Johnson but if he loses he must let her lover escape. Rance agrees and when they have each won a game, Minnie wins the third and deciding one, using cards that she has concealed in her stocking top. As a gambler, Rance keeps to his side of the bargain and after bidding her a curt 'Good night', he leaves.

The third act is set in a clearing in the forest, a few days later. It is dawn and Rance is sitting by a camp fire, talking to Nick. Ashby and some of the miners are also there but asleep on the ground, with their horses tethered nearby. From their conversation, we soon learn that Rance has told Nick of how he lost the poker game and was forced to let Ramerrez escape. Nick says that he wishes that they could go back to the time before Ramerrez came into their lives. He does not mention Minnie but, like the others, he is devoted to her and clearly means that he regrets her infatuation with the bandit. Rance says that he thought Ramerrez's wound would be fatal and curses him. He admits that he longed to reveal where he was hiding and Nick compliments him for resisting the temptation and keeping his word to Minnie.

From out in the forest they hear shots, then some of the miners rush into the clearing to tell them that Ramerrez has been captured. As Ashby prepares to leave with the miners he remarks that he cannot understand why, since the night that Ramerrez was at the Polka, Rance seems to have lost interest in pursuing him. This veiled rebuke, which he cannot answer, increases Rance's hostility towards Ramerrez. When Ashby has gone he tells Nick that he is delighted that the bandit is about to be caught and even takes some pleasure in anticipating Minnie's anguish at learning of her lover's fate. Sonora appears and announces that Ramerrez has been captured. The miners look forward to lynching him and a noose is prepared. Nick immediately hurries off to tell Minnie what has happened.

Johnson is brought in, bound and bleeding from the wound he received on the night of the poker game, and Ashby hands him over to Rance. The Sheriff joins the miners in taunting the prisoner and, in reply to their accusations, he admits that he has been a bandit but swears that he has never committed a murder. He says he is ready to die but wishes first to speak to the girl he loves. This increases the miners' hostility and they tell him he has stolen Minnie's affections. They clamour for him to be hanged immediately but, although he loves Minnie, Sonora objects. He protests that the man has the right to speak.

Johnson asks them to kill him quickly but to tell Minnie that he has gone off to lead the sort of honest life she would have wished for him. This enrages Rance and he strikes Johnson viciously and despite their feelings the miners mutter angrily at seeing him do this to a bound captive. There is no objection from them, however, when the noose is placed round Johnson's neck. He is about to stand on the stones that the miners have piled beneath the noose when they hear Minnie call to them and she rides into the clearing.

Placing herself in front of Johnson, Minnie draws her gun to keep the miners away from him. With Rance frenziedly urging them to go ahead and lynch the bandit, she reminds them of all they owe to her and begs them to spare the life of the man she loves, who now regrets his life of crime. Sonora is the first to be won over and shows his love for Minnie by taking her side. As she throws down her gun he shakes Johnson's hand and the others are persuaded. Johnson is allowed to go but the miners tell him that he must never return. Bidding a sad farewell to California, he and Minnie walk off together, leaving the miners in sorrow that they will never see their 'Girl' again.

It's when Johnson, the tenor lead, thinks that he is about to die that he sings the opera's best-known aria 'Ch'ella mi creda libero e lontano' ('Let her believe me free and far away') which is still occasionally performed on the concert platform. Throughout the opera there are solo passages for the principals, Minnie, Johnson and Rance, and one which Minnie sings towards the end of the first act, when she is disturbed by the feeling that Johnson is invoking in her, is very moving. She sings, 'Io non son che una povera fanciulla' ('I'm only a poor girl, obscure and good for nothing') and later, when she invites him to come to her cabin, she tells him not to expect too much of her. Johnson responds, 'Nothing really matters when you've a good and pure nature, and the face of an angel.'

With *La Bohème* ringing in their ears, some audiences no doubt anticipated a typical Puccini love duet at this point, but it would have been out of place. Rodolfo and Mimi might have declared their undying love a few minutes and a couple of arias after meeting each other but Mimi, although a gentle soul, was used to the ways of the bohemian world in which she lived and would probably have had affairs before she met Rodolfo. To Minnie, it's all new and although she soon finds herself in the situation of having to acknowledge her love for Johnson, this first real meeting between them brings about a pleasurable but disturbing discovery of her womanly feelings. Johnson – and Puccini – would have realised that and the composer and the character both go about things in a subtle and sensitive manner.

Puccini did manage to include a love duet and this comes at the appropriate moment in the second act, when Minnie surrenders to her feeling when Johnson says that he must have a kiss from her. When Rance, Ashby, Nick and Sonora have told her that Johnson is really Ramerrez and she confronts him, he tells her that he was forced to become a bandit in an aria, 'Ma non vi avrei rubato' ('But I wouldn't have robbed you'), which isn't one of Puccini's more memorable ones. The rest of the act is full of incident but there are no more arias or duets, which is in keeping with the fast and dramatic action. Puccini provides suitably exciting music for the wounding of Johnson, Rance's discovery of him in the cabin and Minnie's poker game with Rance. Set pieces – even a spirited duet between Minnie and Rance as they play poker for Johnson's life – would have slowed down the action.

The final act is similar, with Johnson's 'Ch'ella mi creda' providing a very effective lyrical moment after continuous parlando – not to mention giving time for Minnie to come to the scene and save his life. When she arrives, she begins a solo which becomes a general ensemble as she pleads with the miners to spare her lover. The act ends with them singing a folk song, previously heard in Act 1, and Minnie and Johnson walking away singing 'Addio, mia California' ('Farewell, my California').

At the New York premiere of *La Fanciulla del West*, the legendary Enrico Caruso sang the part of Johnson – the only Puccini role that he originated. Minnie was sung by the distinguished Czech soprano Emmy Destinn, who was noted for her acting as well as her singing. The role should have given her scope for both talents but Puccini was not completely happy about the casting. His comment was that she was 'not bad, but she needs more energy'. She could not have been the only Minnie who failed to please him as a few years later he attended a performance in which the Italian soprano Gilda dalla Rizza sang the role and he remarked, 'At last I have seen my Fanciulla.'

At the premiere, the opera was given a rousing reception and press comment was very favourable. Within a few weeks it had been performed in several other American cities, where it was also

well received and it had a successful premiere at Covent Garden in
1911. Its initial popularity in America may have been because it was
the first opera with an American story by a major composer, but in
later years the Wild West setting seemed to make it difficult for some
opera critics to take it seriously. It's certainly true that a photograph
that still exists of Caruso in Western dress, complete with six-guns, is
a little unbelievable. Although there were two mini-revivals in later
decades, its only real success was in those early years and it's now an
almost forgotten work.

It was while he was composing *La Fanciulla del West* that one of
the most unfortunate episodes in Puccini's life took place. Working
as a maidservant in his house at Torre del Lago was a young local
girl, Doria Manfredi. One evening in the autumn of 1908 she was
standing at the door of Puccini's study, talking to him, when Elvira
suddenly appeared and hysterically accused her of having an affair
with him. As it was later proved, there was no truth in this at all
and, as Doria had then been working for them for four years, it
was strange that Elvira should suddenly have suspected her. Elvira,
however, had become very jealous and difficult – jealous because she
was more than justified, and probably more difficult because of it.
On that occasion, she must have become completely irrational.

It's likely that she knew of Puccini's affairs because they were well
known among his associates, but she usually acted as though she
was unaware of them. Having experienced disapproval when she left
her husband for him, however, she no doubt felt that she deserved
greater loyalty from him. It may be that when she accused Doria,
Puccini had been indulging in one of his extramarital liaisons and,
having yet again managed to restrain herself, the sight of him talking
to another woman somehow triggered off her repressed resentment,
but whatever the reason for it may have been, her outburst had tragic
consequences.

With Elvira screaming accusations at her, Doria took refuge in her
room until early the following morning, when she left the house.
Puccini would have tried to convince Elvira of the girl's innocence

but later that day she went round the neighbourhood telling anyone who would listen to her that she had dismissed Doria because she had been carrying on an affair with her husband. The local people might have been sceptical that Doria had behaved in that way but Puccini's reputation with women was well known and, sensing that she was becoming the subject of unpleasant rumours, the unfortunate girl became more and more distraught. Finally, she committed suicide by swallowing disinfectant and suffered several days of agony before she died on 28 January 1909.

Puccini was horrified by the girl's tragic death. He left Elvira, at the time intending to have nothing more to do with her, as he told Sybil Seligman when he wrote to her soon after his departure. A post-mortem examination proved that Doria had been a virgin and the Manfredi family immediately brought a civil action against Elvira for defamation and persecution. It's an indication of her state of mind that in spite of the clear evidence of the girl's innocence she wrote a furious letter to Puccini insisting, 'You know you are guilty.'

The court proceedings ended in July 1909, with Elvira being fined and sentenced to five months' imprisonment. She appealed and Puccini, already on the point of returning to her, managed to negotiate a settlement out of court with the Manfredi family, who eventually accepted a large sum of money as compensation. In September 1909, Puccini had come back to Elvira and with their son Tonio they were living together again at Torre del Lago. He wrote again to Sybil Seligman, telling her of the reconciliation. He said, 'In my house I have peace – Elvira is good – and the three of us live happily together.'

He also mentioned that he had recommended work on *La Fanciulla del West*, saying, 'I've nearly finished the second act – where there's a love duet which seems to me to have come out well.'

This was only about nine months after the horrific death of the innocent girl but Puccini seemed again to be contentedly absorbed in his work and happy that he and Elvira were reunited. As he must have known, he had some responsibility for the tragedy because his past behaviour had probably evoked Elvira's jealousy and caused her irrational suspicions about the girl. His apparent complacency – perhaps even callousness – did not of course mean that there were never any recriminations between him and Elvira in the future or that he was ever able to put the affair completely behind him.

What can be said, however, is that the reconciliation was proof of the genuine feeling between him and Elvira, and his pleasure at how the new opera was turning out shows how a great composer will often have what is practically a second existence, which worldly matters can rarely if ever affect. Puccini was selfish, a womaniser and almost amoral – but, above all those things, a musician.

Above left: 1. *Le Villi*
1884 advert.

Above right and middle:
2 & 3. *La Bohème* props.

Below right: 4. *La
Bohème* Act 2 costume.

5. *Tosca* original libretto.

6. Castel Sant'Angelo.

7. Rosina Storchio.

8. Original poster for *Madama Butterfly*.

Above left: 9. Emmy Destinn.

Above right: 10. Gilda dalla Rizza.

11. *La Fanciulla del West.*

Above left: 12. Tito Schipa.

Above right: 13. Costume for *Il Tabarro.*

14. *Turandot* poster.

9

La Rondine

Libretto by Giuseppe Adami (Adami's Italian libretto was based on one by Alfred Maria Willner and Heinz Reichert)
Opera commissioned by the owners of the Carltheater, Vienna

Premiere – Grand Théâtre de Monte-Carlo, Monaco, 27 March 1917
Conductor – Gino Marinuzzi

CAST

Magda de Civry	Soprano	Gilda dalla Rizza
Lisette, her maid	Soprano	Ines Maria Ferraris
Ruggero Lastouc	Tenor	Tito Schipa
Prunier, a poet	Tenor	Francesco Dominici
Rambaldo Fernandez, Magda's protector	Baritone	Gustave Huberdeau
Périchaud	Baritone	Libert
Gobin	Tenor	Charles Delmas
Crébillon	Baritone	Stéphane
Rabonnier	Baritone	
Yvette	Soprano	Suzy Laugée
Bianca	Soprano	Andrée Moreau
Suzy	Mezzo-Soprano	Charlotte Mattei
A Butler	Bass	Delestan

La Rondine, Puccini's eighth opera, was the only one that was not published by Casa Ricordi, the Milan publishing house founded by Giulio Ricordi, Puccini's 'Papa Giulio' who had been his been his mentor throughout his career. Giulio Ricordi died in 1912 and his son Tito declined to publish *La Rondine* – in a letter that he wrote to Sybil Seligman, Puccini said that the publisher had called it 'bad Lehár' and an opera that had failed to 'come off'. Franz Lehár was a Hungarian-born composer of successful operettas such as *The Merry Widow*. They were pleasing and popular works, but decidedly lightweight in comparison with Puccini's operas and the description would not have pleased him.

There had never been any open hostility between the two men, but there may have been some personal feeling in this. The remark suggested that although the younger Ricordi would not have turned down a work because of enmity, he was glad of a reason to do so on professional grounds. For his part, it was known that Puccini resented Ricordi's autocratic attitude, often referring to him as 'Savoia' – the name of the then ruling house in Italy. Giulio Ricordi would certainly have been a lot more tactful and, if he had found *La Rondine* to be lacking in any way, he would probably have been pleased to offer suggestions as to how it might be improved. Puccini offered the work to the rival publisher, Lorenzo Sonzogno, who was pleased to accept it.

Puccini had actually thought about writing a traditional operetta, a humorous work in which there is a lot of spoken dialogue, whereas in an opera all dialogue is sung. The possibility came closer when he was in Vienna in 1913 for a performance of *La Fanciulla del West* and two Austrian theatre directors, Heinrich Berté and Otto Eibenschütz, made him a highly lucrative offer to write an operetta for them. A libretto was prepared but Puccini was unimpressed by it and, according to a letter that he wrote to a friend soon afterwards, he seemed then to have abandoned any thought of writing an operetta. Soon afterwards, however, Berté and Eibenschütz offered him the libretto of another operetta and Puccini accepted it after reading only one act – but with the intention of turning it into a standard opera, with only sung dialogue. The original libretto had been written in German, by Alfred Maria Willner and Heinz Reichert, and it was translated into Italian by Giuseppe Adami, a young Veronese playwright. Giulio Ricordi had introduced him to Puccini a few years earlier, in connection with one of the many projects that he considered for a while but then abandoned.

The heroine of *La Rondine* is Magda de Civry, the mistress of Rambaldo Fernandez, a rich Parisian banker. It's a comfortable existence for her but she is beginning to tire of purely material comforts. When the opera opens she is entertaining some guests at Rambaldo's house and it interests her when one of them, a poet named Prunier, says that in Paris romantic love is becoming an 'epidemic of madness, affecting the female population'. When he attempts some palmistry, he predicts that Magda will one day 'fly to the south, like the Swallow [*Rondine*] in search of true love'.

After Magda has helped Pruinier to complete a song that he is writing, Ruggero Lastouc, the son of one of Rambaldo's friends, comes to the house. He is on his first visit and the guests try to decide where he should spend his first evening. Magda suggests the nearby Bullier's Restaurant, where she once had a youthful flirtation that she has never been able to forget. When her guests have gone, she disguises herself as a *grisette* (working girl) and, after reassuring herself by murmuring, 'Who would ever recognise me?', she goes out.

The second act is set in Bullier's Restaurant. Ruggero has attracted the attention of some *grisettes* and, being very inexperienced, he does not realise that he is being giving the 'come on'; he is merely embarrassed by their advances. Magda comes in, introduces herself as Paulette and asks Ruggero if she may join him. He fails to recognise her, unlike Prunier, who also comes to the restaurant, escorting Magda's maid Lisette, with whom he is having an affair. Lisette also recognises Magda but Prunier manages to convince her that she is mistaken when Magda asks him not to reveal her identity. The two couples spend the evening together and Ruggero becomes more and more infatuated with Magda, who is really trying to recreate the romantic episode in her youth, in the same restaurant.

By the sort of coincidence which only occurs in opera, Rambaldo also comes to the restaurant. Prunier sees him come in and warns Magda, who begs him to help her. She knows that Rambaldo will recognise her and that if he speaks to her Ruggero will realise who she is. She is desperate to prevent that and Prunier thinks of a plan. He asks Ruggero to take Lisette out, telling him that her employer has come to the restaurant and will be angry if he sees her there. Ruggero agrees and he and Lisette leave. When Rambaldo comes over to ask Magda what she is doing there she tells him that she has found a new love and their relationship is over. Rambaldo tries to dissuade her but, seeing that she is adamant, he bids her a sad and dignified farewell. Magda is left alone, listening to a girl singing in the street outside, until Ruggero returns and they pledge their love for each other.

The third act takes place on the terrace of a villa on the French Riviera, where Magda and Ruggero are now living together. Ruggero is very happy and tells Magda that he has written to his father, asking for his consent to them marrying. When he leaves her, Magda is uneasy because she realises that when they know of her past his family will never accept her. Prunier arrives with Lisette, who is very unhappy. He has encouraged her to attempt a theatrical career but on her debut the previous evening she was booed from the stage. She has come to ask Magda to take her back as her maid. Magda agrees and Lisette goes off to change into her uniform.

Before he leaves, Prunier tells Magda that Rambaldo would be pleased if she returned to him and he makes the point that Lisette is much happier now that she is no longer trying to be something that she is not. Ruggero comes in, delighted because he has received a letter from his mother, giving him her blessing for his proposed marriage – but as Magda knows, this is on the assumption that his bride is a young and pure maiden. She now realises that her escapade has gone too far. She tells Ruggero the truth about herself and says that she must leave him so that one day he can find a wife suitable for him, and whom his family will accept. With Lisette in attendance, she makes a sad exit as the heartbroken Ruggero collapses tearfully into a chair.

Puccini's original agreement with Berté and Eibenschütz was that *La Rondine* would have its premiere in Vienna and for that occasion it would be translated into German. This never happened because by the time the opera was completed in 1916 the First World War had begun and Italy and Austria were on different sides. Lorenzo Sonzogno suggested that the premiere should be in Monte Carlo, and it took place there in March 1917. The part of Magda was sung by Gilda dalla Rizza, thought to be Puccini's favourite soprano, for whom he created the role. It was one of thirteen that she originated in her career.

The role of Magda is a very demanding one in respect of acting as well as singing, and by far the most important in *La Rondine*, but apart from two arias in the first act neither she nor Ruggero have any memorable solo pieces. As in *Madama Butterfly* and *La Fanciulla del West* Puccini made his solos and ensembles integral parts of the action, rather than show-stoppers. Magda's first aria is early in the first act, when she improvises an ending for a song that Prunier is writing. 'Chi il bel sogno di Doretta' ('The beautiful dream of Doretta') is about a girl named Doretta who dreams of a prince, and later in 'Ore dolci e divine' ('Divine and times') she recalls her youthful experience in the restaurant. A completely innovative touch that Puccini gave to the opera was to use modern dance rhythms as themes for the various characters. Prunier's, for example, was a tango.

The opera was well received in Monte Carlo and soon afterwards in Buenos Aires, with its large Italian community as usual eager to attend operas. It failed to raise much enthusiasm in Italy, however, and possibly as a consequence it was quite a while before it was performed in other centres. The first New York performance, with the famous tenor Beniamino Gigli as Ruggero, was not until 1928, some eleven years after the Monte Carlo premiere. It was never performed at Covent Garden although Sybil Seligman negotiated with the management with a view to having a production there. Puccini finally declined their offer, mainly because they had wanted spoken dialogue included.

Although the ending was a sad one, *La Rondine*, like *La Fanciulla del West* before it, detracts from the belief that Puccini was drawn to themes involving violence, torture and death. That might be said of many composers – Verdi's *Rigoletto* had a particularly tragic end, involving the death of its heroine, and he also based operas on the Shakespearean tragedies *Macbeth* and *Othello*. The truth is probably that, like many of his fellow composers, Puccini was mainly concerned that a story would translate successfully into an opera. His contretemps with Leoncavallo over *La Bohème* suggests that there could be quite ruthless competition over the rights to such stories.

In that *La Rondine* was such a bold, innovative venture for Puccini, as he must have known, it seems that he was far less concerned with commercial success than his critics often suggest. True to form, he made several revisions to the work, but it has been said, aptly, that in box office terms it was 'the poor cousin' of his greater hits. It is, however, quite regularly revived in Great Britain, the USA and even Finland, and in 2002 there was a production at Convent Garden with the famous Romanian soprano Angela Gheorghiu singing the part of Magda. Further indication of the respect that it has received from celebrated singers was a 1981 recording with Kiri Te Kanawa and Plácido Domingo in the lead roles.

10

Il Trittico

Premiere – Metropolitan House, New York, 14 December 1918
Conductor – Roberto Moranzoni

Il Trittico, a triple bill of one-act operas, was first performed in December 1918, less than two years after *La Rondine* had its premiere. That was a very short interval between Puccini's operas but he had worked on the two productions together, shelving *Il Trittico* when *La Rondine* had reached the rehearsal stage and was taking up most of his time. After the premiere he resumed work on *Il Trittico*, and enough of it had been written for him to be able to complete it fairly quickly.

Puccini gave the three operas the title *Trittico* for want of a better one. It means 'triptych', which is actually a term for three pictures or carvings with a common theme, fixed or hinged together. He had begun planning a collection of one-act operas in 1904, possibly because of the success of his friend Pietro Mascagni's *Cavalleria Rusticana*. He had originally intended that all three operas should echo parts of Dante's *Divine Comedy* but in the end only one of them was based on the poem. That was the third, and the most popular of them, *Gianni Schicchi*. The others were chosen purely for their appeal and suitability for operas. The term 'triptych' was therefore inappropriate because there was no common theme for the three.

Il Tabarro

Libretto by Giuseppe Adami
Based on *La Houppelande*, a play by Didier Gold

CAST

Michele, a barge owner	Baritone	Luigi Montesanto
Giorgetta, Michele's wife	Soprano	Claudia Muzio
Luigi, a stevedore	Tenor	Giulio Crimi
'Tinca' ('Tench'), a stevedore	Tenor	Angelo Badà
'Talpa' ('Mole'), a stevedore	Bass	Adamo Didur
La Frugola, ('The Rummager'), Talpa's wife	Mezzo-Soprano	Alice Gentle

Il Tabarro (*The Cloak*) was based on a play by the French dramatist Didier Gold. The librettist was Giuseppe Adami, who completed work on that part of the triple bill before he began to write the libretto of *La Rondine*. He took over from Ferdinand Martini, an elderly writer who gave up the task when Puccini, in one of his impatient moods, pressed him to work faster.

The story of *Il Tabarro* is a simple one of love, jealousy and revenge, set on a barge moored on the River Seine in Paris, in the early part of the twentieth century. Michele, the middle-aged barge owner, and his much younger wife Giorgetta, once had a child, who died. As the story opens, Michele feels that Giorgetta is growing cold towards him and suspects, rightly, that she has a lover. This is Luigi, the youngest of three stevedores who come to the barge to unload it. Michele finds out the truth accidentally, when he stands on the deck of the barge at night and strikes a match to light his pipe. Luigi, watching nearby, sees the flame and thinking that this is Giorgetta's signal that the coast is clear, makes his way stealthily on board. Michele pounces on Luigi and forces him to confess that he is Giorgetta's lover, then strangles him and hides body under his large cloak. Giorgetta comes up on deck and senses hostility in Michele's manner. To placate him, she asks him to take her under his cloak to shield her from the cold river breezes, as he used to do when they were first in love. Michele takes sadistic pleasure in opening the cloak and forcing her to come face to face with her dead lover.

The rather sombre story is relieved by some lighter moments, provided by some minor characters. Before it grows dark, Luigi and the other two stevedores, Tinca ('Tench') and Talpa ('Mole'), are unloading the barge when Giorgetta brings them some wine. Michele refuses to join them as Giorgetta has just refused his kiss. From onshore the sound of an organ grinder is heard and the three men start to dance to the music. When one of them steps on Giorgetta's foot, Luigi dances with her and the feeling between them becomes obvious. When Michele appears, the three men go back to work.

Michele tells Giorgetta that work is scarce and one of the stevedores will have to be laid off. Giorgetta gives further indication of the feeling between her and Luigi by insisting that it should be one of the others, and she and Michele start to argue. Talpa's wife, called La Frugola ('The Rummager'), comes on board, looking for him and shows everyone the things she has obtained from scavenging in Paris. She becomes angry with the men when she realises that they have been drinking but then sings of how she longs one day to buy a house in the country, so that she and Talpa can retire and live there.

Giorgetta and Luigi sing nostalgically together about the town where they were both born, then, when Talpa and Tinca have gone, Luigi is left alone with Michele. He asks Michele to dismiss him so that he can leave the barge in Rouen, but Michele dissuades him. This is probably a ploy because, when they are alone, Giorgetta asks Luigi why he asked to be dismissed and he tells her that he cannot share her with Michele. She agrees that it is a 'torment' and they declare their love for each other. This is when they arrange to meet later that evening, when Giorgetta lights a match to tell Luigi that it is safe to come aboard. Luigi then seems ready to kill Michele and go off with Giorgetta.

The final scene is short, with Luigi coming on board when Michele strikes the match and being killed by him, after a brief confrontation. This is preceded by a brief scene between Michele and Giorgetta, in which she again refuses his kiss. In one version of the opera Michele had a rather sombre aria, 'Flow on eternal river', but this was one of several changes that over the years Puccini made, in his usual way, as he tried to improve the work.

True to his verismo approach, and with the opera a short one, he included only a few set pieces. It has been recorded quite regularly with distinguished singers such as Tito Gobbi and Renata Tebaldi taking part, but *Il Tabarro* is rarely staged. Individually, the three operas comprising *Il Trittico* were all considered competent enough, but it was soon obvious that they would not catch on as a triple bill. If they were staged individually it was necessary to find other operas to put on with them to provide a full programme. Mascagni's *Cavalleria Rusticana* and Leoncavallo's *Pagliacci* have always been favourites, but *Il Tabarro* had not the appeal of either and consequently has never found a regular partner.

Suor Angelica

Libretto by Giovacchino Forzano
Based on a play by Forzano

CAST

Sister Angelica	Soprano	Geraldine Farrar
The Princess, her aunt	Contralto	Flora Perini
The Abbess	Mezzo-Soprano	Rita Fornia
The Monitress	Mezzo-Soprano	Marie Sundelius
The Mistress of the Novices	Mezzo-Soprano	Cecil Arden
Sister Genovieffa	Soprano	Mary Ellis
Sister Osmina	Soprano	Margarete Belleri
Sister Dolcina	Soprano	Marie Mattfeld
The Nursing Sister	Mezzo-Soprano	Leonora Sparkes

Alms Sister	Soprano	Kitty Beale
Alms Sister	Soprano	Minnie Egener
A Novice	Soprano	Phillis White
Lay Sister	Soprano	Marie Tiffany
Lay Sister	Mezzo-Soprano	Veni Warwick

Il Tabarro had already been written when Puccini returned to work on his triple bill and he quickly decided upon the two operas that he needed to complete it. In both cases, the libretti were provided by Giovacchino Forzano, a stage director of his acquaintance. Trained as a baritone, Forzano appeared in a number of provincial operatic productions and he also wrote libretti for several composers, including Leoncavallo and Puccini's friend from his student days, Pietro Mascagni.

When Puccini began looking for the two additional stories, Forzano was planning a one-act play, *Sua Angelica* (*Sister Angelica*). He read the storyline to Puccini, who immediately saw its potential as an opera and invited Forzano to collaborate with him. Forzano agreed and within a few weeks he had completed the libretto, which Puccini was pleased to accept. Unless he simply thought it an unusually good libretto, this change from Puccini's earlier behaviour toward his collaborators might have been because he was then established as a major composer and, with the failure of *Edgar* well behind him, he was able to approach his operas with greater confidence.

Set in a convent at the end of the seventeenth century, Forzano's story is of Angelica, a nun who was sent there by her aristocratic family seven years earlier when she had disgraced them by having an illegitimate baby. Her hopes that they will one day forgive her are raised when she receives a visit from her elderly aunt 'La Zia Principessa' – but she is quickly disappointed. Angelica's younger sister is about to marry and the old lady has come to ask her to sign a document renouncing her inheritance in the sister's favour. She misses no opportunity to remind Angelica of the shame that she brought on the family.

Angelica agrees to her aunt's request, then asks for news of her little son, who was taken from her at birth. Showing a rare trace of humanity, the aunt is reluctant to tell her that the child died from a fever two years earlier and Angelica collapses. She recovers and obediently signs the paper that her aunt has brought but rejects the old lady's belated attempt at a gesture of affection. Still shocked, she begins to experience a strange feeling of euphoria and imagines herself to be in a state of grace. Believing that she should join her child in heaven, she uses the expert knowledge of herbs that she has acquired during her years in the convent to make herself a poison.

Having swallowed it, she realises that she had committed a mortal sin and prays for forgiveness. As she dies she is comforted by a vision in which the doors of the convent chapel open, showing a building filled with a brilliant light, in the midst of which her child is standing with the Virgin Mary, who pushes the boy into the dying Angelica's arms. A chorus of nuns sing 'Thou art saved', signifying that Angelica is pardoned.

This is the basic storyline of the opera but it is preceded by minor incidents involving Angelica and the other nuns, with Angelica's herbal knowledge revealed. For a short opera, it has a large cast – all female – with twelve other members of the convent, from the Abbess down to a novice and two lay sisters involved. With only one full aria, Angelica's 'Senza mama' ('Without a mother') as she laments the death of her child, *Suor Angelica* was the least popular of the three operas, although Puccini, in a defensive mood when it was once suggested that *Il Trittico* should be performed without it, claimed it was the best.

It was not long, however, before he had to admit that his idea of a triple bill had not worked and when the three operas were staged separately – often as double bills with works of other composers – *Suor Angelica* was rarely performed. There have been some fairly recent recordings – Joan Sutherland sang the part of Angelica on a 1973 version – and one in 1975 included Marilyn Horn, who was the voice of Carmen Jones in the 1954 film version of Oscar Hammerstein's ingenious adaptation of the Bizet opera.

Gianni Schicchi

Libretto by Giovacchino Forzano
Based on lines from Dante's *Inferno*

CAST

Gianni Schicchi	Baritone	Giuseppe de Luca
Lauretta, his daughter	Soprano	Florence Easton
Zita, cousin of Buoso Donati	Contralto	Kathleen Howard
Rinuccio, Zita's nephew	Tenor	Giulio Crimi
Gherardo, Buoso's nephew	Tenor	Angelo Badà
Nella, Gherardo's wife	Soprano	Marie Tiffany
Gherardino, their son	Soprano	Mario Malatesta
Betto di Signa, Buoso's brother-in-law	Bass	Paolo Ananian
Simone, cousin of Buoso	Bass	Adamo Didur
Marco, Simone's son	Baritone	Louis D'Angel
La Ciesca, Marco's wife	Mezzo-Soprano	Marie Sundelius
Maestro Spinelloccio, a doctor	Bass	Pompilio Malatesta
Ser Amantio di Nicolao, a notary	Baritone	Andrés De Segurola
Pinellino, a cobbler	Bass	Vincenzo Reschiglian
Guccio, a dyer	Bass	Carl Schlegel

The idea for *Gianni Schicchi*, the third opera of *Il Trittico*, occurred to Forzano when he was reading Dante's *Inferno*. He suggested it to Puccini, who was immediately taken with the idea – perhaps because of his original intention of basing all three operas on parts of Dante's poem. The libretto was quickly completed.

Gianni Schicchi was probably a real character who lived in Florence in the thirteenth century – the opera is set in the year 1299. A kind of Arthur Daley character, he and other newcomers brought wealth to the city but some of the traditional families of Florence regarded them as vulgar upstarts and interlopers. In Dante's poem he is encountered in Hell, having been condemned for forging a will to cheat a family named Donati out of an inheritance. It's believed that Dante's wife was a member of the Donati family, so this may actually have happened.

The opera opens with the Donatis assembling at the house of their wealthy relative Buoso, who has just died. They are worried by a rumour that he has left all his estate to the local monastery – and when they find the will, they see that it is true. Rinuccio, one of the younger members of the family, is in love with Gianni Schicchi's daughter Lauretta and, anxious to establish good relations between his family and hers, he suggests that Schicchi might help them. Knowing his humble origins, the family are not very happy about involving Schicchi in their affairs, and say that marriage to the daughter of a peasant is unthinkable but in the aria 'Avete torto' ('You are mistaken') Rinuccio defends him. The family then begin to argue among themselves, and Rinuccio takes advantage of the confusion to send off one of the younger relations to Schicchi to tell him to come to the house.

Schicchi arrives with Lauretta but quickly tells the Donatis to find their own solution when he is insulted by Rinuccio's aunt Zita, also called La Vecchia ('The Old Woman'), who is now seen as the head of the family. Lauretta is distraught because she knows that in spite of his successful business dealings, Schicchi will be unable to give her a large marriage dowry and that unless the family can find some way of inheriting Buoso's money, Zito will not allow Rinuccio to marry her.

She begs Schicchi to stay and help the family in what has become one of Puccini's most popular arias, 'O mio babbino caro' ('Oh my dear Papa') – since recorded by practically every leading soprano. In it, Lauretta assures her father that she loves Rinuccio and says that if she cannot marry him, she will go to Florence's famous bridge the Ponte Vecchio and throw herself in the river. Schicchi probably realises that the Arno isn't very deep by the bridge but he agrees to give his assistance.

Schicchi sends Lauretta out so that she will be innocent of what he is about to do. He has the corpse removed from the bed, then sends for Buoso's doctor and outlines his plans in the aria 'Si corre dal notaio' ('Run to the notary'). With three of the women helping him – 'Spogliati, bambolino' ('Undress little boy') – he disguises himself as Buoso so that when the notary comes, he will dictate a new will. As he puts on the disguise several members of the family come to him and offer bribes if he will favour them with particular bequests in the will.

Schicchi hides behinds the bed curtains when the doctor arrives. Imitating Buoso's voice, he says that he is feeling better than he did when the doctor last saw him, but asks him to come back in the evening – when he does, he will be shown the body of Buoso and told that he has only just died. When the doctor has gone the notary then arrives and Schicchi starts to dictate the new will, first of all making reasonable bequests to Zita and other relations. He then moves on to the three most coveted items, which are Buoso's house, his mule – said to be the best in Tuscany – and some mills at the town of Signa.

He tells the notary that the mule is to be left to 'my devoted friend Gianni Schicchi'. The Donatis are appalled but from behind the curtains, Schicchi waves the empty sleeve of Buoso's nightshirt and sings 'Addio Firenze' ('Farewell, Florence') – reminding them that in Florence the penalty for falsifying a will is amputation of the right hand and banishment from the city. As they are implicated, they cannot protest and Schicchi goes on to leave himself the house and the mills.

When the notary has gone, the furious relatives accuse Schicchi of stealing their property and, as the house is now his, he orders them out. They leave, frantically grabbing anything of value that they see as they go. Lauretta and Rinuccio are delighted and sing a duet, 'Lauretta mia, staremo sempre qui!' ('Lauretta mine, here we'll always stay!'). Schicchi then goes to the footlights and appeals to the audience. Dante condemned him to Hell for taking Buoso's property but he did it to make two young lovers happy and he cannot think of a better reason. He feels sure that the audience will agree that there was mitigation and he encourages them to show this by applauding.

Puccini had hoped that *Il Trittico* would have its premiere in Rome, but in the aftermath of the Great War this was not possible. It was first staged in New York in December 1914, only a few weeks after hostilities had ended. Puccini was unable to attend because of travel restrictions and the Atlantic crossing was considered dangerous because of mines. It was received politely but even at that stage it seemed likely that, of the three operas, only *Gianni Schicchi* was likely to arouse any enthusiasm. Puccini was angered at attempts to separate the three for performances but eventually had to admit that *Il Trittico* could not survive as a triple bill. He may have been consoled by the fact that in *Gianni Schicchi* he had established that he was master of comedy as well as tragedy.

11

Turandot

Libretto by Giuseppe Adami and Renato Simoni
Based on *Turandot* a play by Carlo Gozzi

Premiere – Teatro della Scala, Milan, 25 April 1926
Conductor – Arturo Toscanini

CAST

Princess Turandot	Soprano	Rosa Raisa
Emperor Altoum, her father	Tenor	Francesco Dominici
Timur, deposed king of Tartary	Bass	Carlo Walter
The Unknown Prince (Calàf), Timur's son	Tenor	Miguel Fleta
Liù, a slave girl	Soprano	Maria Zamboni
Ping, Lord Chancellor	Baritone	Giacomo Rimini
Pang, Majordomo	Tenor	Emilio Venturini
Pong, Chief Chef	Tenor	Giuseppe Nessi
A Mandarin	Baritone	Aristide Baracchi
The Prince of Persia	Tenor	
Pu-Tin-Pao, the executioner	Silent	

Giacomo Puccini died on 28 November 1924, in Brussels, where he was undergoing treatment for cancer of the throat. The disease was probably the legacy of his early addiction to smoking which began when he was still at school. After his death, a poem was found among his papers, on a page dated 3 March 1923. In its Italian form the poem had very little punctuation, as if he wrote it in a preoccupied way, as his thoughts came to him, and it reads the same way in English. He wrote:

> I have no friends, I feel alone
> Even music makes me sad
> When death comes to find me
> I shall be happy to rest
> Oh how hard is my life
> Though to many I seem happy
> But my successes pass
> And ... what remains?
> It's worth little
> They are ephemeral things
> Life runs on towards the abyss
> He who lives and is young
> finds the world enjoyable
> but who is aware of this?
> It passes quickly, one's youth
> and the eye scrutinises eternity.

With his talk of the passing of youth and looking into eternity, it would be easy to believe that the poem was the expression of some sort of premonition. As early as 1908, when he mentioned it in a letter to Sybil Seligman, Puccini had suffered from a persistent soreness of the throat which made his voice almost permanently hoarse. It may be that he had felt moved to write the poem in 1923 because the condition has worsened, warning him of a potentially fatal disease, but he was also worried about the lack of progress on his latest opera and, as he often was at such times, he probably felt generally depressed. Later in the year, when work had recommenced, his spirits seemed to revive but by the autumn of 1924, not long before he died, he was showing great impatience to complete the opera, almost as if he sensed that his time was limited. That opera, which he never quite completed but is considered to be one of his finest, was *Turandot*.

After the completion of *Il Trittico*, Puccini began the usual process of searching for a theme for his next production and toying with various ideas which, after varying degrees of enthusiasm, he abandoned. At one time he seemed quite committed to the idea of writing an opera around Nancy, in *Oliver Twist*. Dickens was one of his favourite authors and, of course, Nancy comes to a tragic end at the hands of her lover, Bill Sikes. Her name would have been changed to Fanny, which would have been the title of the opera. It was not long, however, before that idea went the same way as so many that had temporarily appealed to him.

Working with Puccini at that time were Giuseppe Adami, who wrote the libretti for *La Rondine* and *Il Tabarro*, and Renato Simoni, a critic and playwright, who had succeeded Giuseppe Giacosa as editor of a review journal, *La Lettura*. With a view to finally deciding on his next opera, Puccini arranged a meeting with them in Milan, in March 1920, and it was while they were having lunch that Simoni suggested to him that *Turandot* would be a suitable subject. The drama or 'modern fable' on which the opera would be based was by Count Carlo Gozzi (1720–1806) and the story was probably familiar to Simoni as a few years earlier he had written a play about Gozzi.

The idea was discussed for a while but when the three men parted Puccini had made no decision about it. A few days later, however, Simoni received a letter from him, setting out his ideas on the structure of the new opera and asking him and Adami to begin work on a libretto. Puccini would have known the story as it had already been used by other operatic composers, including his old tutor Bazzini, and he had obviously thought intensely about it since the meeting in Milan. Having worked with him before, Adami would have known about Puccini's sudden but short-lived bursts of enthusiasm and he may have wondered if this would be yet another false start. Fortunately it was not. Whether he had had some instinctive feeling about it or he was simply anxious to begin a new project, Puccini had made his decision and from then until he died *Turandot* was almost constantly in his mind.

The writing of the new opera, like that of many of his earlier works, proved to be a long and tortuous business. Writing to Sybil Seligman in July 1920, four months after the work had begun, Puccini mentioned that he had still not received the libretto and it was not until January of the following year that he was able to begin composing the score. Three months later he reported to Adami that he was making good progress but, as he often did, he constantly changed his mind about the structure and other facets of the opera and there were periods during the next two years when he seemed to be filled with uncertainty as to whether he was going in the right direction. After the decisiveness that he had shown in completing the second and third operas of *Il Trittico*, this regression to his old ways of uncertainty adds to the feeling that Puccini felt that he had only limited time left – perhaps he was anxious that if this was to be his last offering it should be as near to perfection as he could make it.

In November 1922, he wrote to Adami, informing him that the first act was complete but, 'There isn't a ray to pierce the gloom which shrouds the rest. Perhaps it is wrapped forever in impenetrable darkness. I have a feeling that we shall have to put this work to one side.'

Four months later, his pessimism seemed to have subsided a little when he again wrote to Adami, this time to report that he was working again but, 'I don't say full steam ahead.' He also said that *Turandot* was proving 'a frightful bore' to him and 'We can imagine what it will be to the public.'

A few months later, in the autumn, his enthusiasm seemed to have returned and he had returned to work, despite a certain amount of discomfort that his throat was causing him. This new determination remained with him into 1924 and by the summer of that year, when he was waiting for the verses for the final act, he was clearly becoming impatient. He complained to Adami that he was bored because 'idleness does not suit me'.

In September, he was pressing the librettists for the words for the final duet between the imperious Princess Turandot, from whom the opera takes its name, and the Prince, who finally wins her and shows her true love. He saw them as 'two almost superhuman beings' and wanted it to be 'a great duet'. He received the words in October and was pleased with them, although he felt that there might have to be some alterations to Turandot's part. He mentioned this in a letter of acknowledgement to Adami but added, 'We shall see – when I get back to work again on my return from Brussels.'

The reason for Puccini's visit to Brussels was that a specialist in Florence had found that, contrary to the opinions of a local doctor and another specialist who had seen nothing alarming about the increasing pain in his throat, it was being caused by a growth. Other doctors were consulted and it was recommended that he should have a course of radium treatment at the Institut de Couronne in Brussels, where the resident doctors were experienced in that type of therapy. The condition was thought to be incurable but it was hoped that the spread of the cancer could be delayed for a while. Puccini was never told the full extent of his illness but when he was in the hospital in Brussels, waiting for the treatment to begin, he wrote to a friend saying that he was sceptical about the doctors' assurances that he would be cured.

Tonio Puccini travelled to Brussels with his father but Elvira was ill with bronchitis and had to remain at Viareggio, where they were then living. Fosca, Puccini's stepdaughter, joined him in Brussels on 23 November, the day before the doctors were due to operate. This would have heartened him as he had admitted to being terrified at the thought of the treatment, which was to open his throat to expose the growth and drive seven radioactive needles into it. They were to remain there for seven days, during which he would be fed through a tube.

The operation was duly carried out and after four days the doctors were very optimistic about the result. On the evening of 26 November, Fosca began a letter to Sybil Seligman, reporting that the swelling in her father's throat had disappeared as the radium had destroyed the tumours. The letter was never finished because she was interrupted by a message that Puccini had suffered a heart attack. He died at four o'clock the following morning.

To the opera-loving Italians Puccini had become a national hero and when his body was brought back for burial, it was to a country in mourning. Flags were flown at half-mast and the heavy rain which fell during the funeral service at Milan Cathedral must have seemed appropriate – the tears of a grieving nation. Toscanini conducted the chorus and orchestra of La Scala as, at his suggestion, they performed a requiem from *Edgar* and a soprano sang the aria 'Farewell, farewell my sweet love' from the same opera. Pietro Mascagni, whose friendship with Puccini began in their student days, gave an oration. Puccini lay in Toscanini's family vault in Milan for two years while a mausoleum was being constructed in the family's villa at Torre del Lago.

Turandot was completed by the experienced composer Franco Alfano, who used sketches which Puccini had made. The premiere took place at La Scala on 25 April 1926, but on that occasion Toscanini ended the performance when the last part of Puccini's own score had been reached and announced to the audience that at that point 'the Maestro' had died.

There are many versions of Toscanini's exact words and various interpretations of his motives. At the time it was seen as a moving and appropriate tribute to Puccini, but some biographers have suggested that it was also intended as a snub to Alfano.

Toscanini had involved himself in the completion of *Turandot* – a fact that was obviously unknown to a journalist who, many years later, interpreted his concluding the premiere at the end of Puccini's score as a sign that he disapproved of the posthumous completion of the opera. He and Tonio Puccini had disagreed over the choice of composer to complete the opera and he finally accepted Alfano as a compromise. Relations between the conductor and the composer were often difficult during the final rehearsals but Toscanini was always a perfectionist and it's likely that he was particularly hard to please over *Turandot*.

His genius as a conductor lay in his great talent for interpretation and he would have had a very clear idea of how the opera should be completed as Puccini had discussed it with him shortly before leaving for Brussels. Puccini's plea of 'Don't let my *Turandot* die' may be another indication of premonitions of death. Toscanini conducted *Turandot* complete with Alfano's ending on the next two nights after the premiere, so on balance it seems that on that first occasion he was moved by nothing more than deference to Puccini. To have used the tribute, even partly, to imply criticism of Alfano would have been unworthy and a man of Toscanini's integrity would have realised that.

Alfano, of course, had taken on what was always likely to be a thankless task. It was inevitable that his work would be put under the microscope when the experts, real and self-styled, compared his ending with what they imagined Puccini would have made of it. It has been argued that *Turandot* should have been allowed to end at the point that Puccini had reached when he died and if some people enjoy it less for knowing that it isn't *all* Puccini, this is quite understandable. Others might feel that without Alfano's ending it would be rather like a 'whodunnit' with the final chapter missing – and a close look at the storyline of the opera suggests that they would probably be right.

Turandot is like an Arabian Nights tale, but set in China, in the 'legendary past'. The Princess Turandot has said that she will only marry a suitor who solves her three riddles or enigmas, and those who fail to answer them will be beheaded. As she sends the latest of her unsuccessful challengers to his execution, she is seen by Calàf, the son of Timur, the deposed king of the Tartars. Calàf has led a fugitive life since his father's throne was usurped and never discloses his true identity. He is reunited with Timur, now old and blind, and his faithful slave girl Liù as they stand in the crowd in Peking, waiting for the execution. Smitten by Turandot's beauty, he decides to take up her challenge. Liù (who loves him), Timur and three of Turandot's courtiers, Ping, Pang and Pong, all try to dissuade him but Calàf is determined and he strikes the great gong, committing himself to meet Turandot's challenge.

Before the contest, Ping, Pang and Pong talk together and recall the executions of foreign princes that have taken place since Turandot set her challenge. Twelve unsuccessful suitors have already been beheaded in that year – the Year of the Tiger – and the three courtiers all expect this latest challenger to meet the same fate. As they agree that it would be better for China if a challenger solved the enigmas and so ended the gruesome ritual, a fanfare of trumpets tells them that the trial is about to start.

The contest takes place within the Royal Palace. At the top of a marble staircase is the throne of the Emperor Altoum, the father of Turandot. When the three Wise Men who will act as judges have taken their places, followed by Ping, Pang and Pong, Altoum enters and seats himself on the throne. Calàf comes to the foot of the staircase and Altoum addresses him. Regretfully, he tells him that he is bound by an oath to keep the condition that those who fail to solve the enigmas must die. Three times he urges the stranger to abandon his challenge but Calàf's answer is always the same. Respectfully but firmly he tells the Emperor that he still wishes to undergo the test.

The conditions of the contest are then announced and Turandot, standing at her father's side, adds her warning. She believes herself to be the reincarnation of her ancestress the Princess Lo-u-Ling, who many centuries earlier was ravished and murdered when China was invaded by a foreign army. Her purpose in life is to avenge Lo-u-Ling and she will never allow a man to possess her. She tells Calàf that 'the enigmas are three, but death is one'. Calàf replies, 'No, the enigmas are three, *life* is one.'

Turandot then puts the first enigma to him:

In the dark, an iridescent phantom lies. It spreads its wings and soars above the black infinity of mankind. The whole world invokes and implores it, but the phantom vanishes at dawn, to be reborn in the heart. Every night it is born, every day it dies.

Calàf answers almost immediately, 'Yes, it is born again and carries me away in rapture. Turandot, the answer is hope.' The Wise Men confirm that he is right. Turandot moves halfway down the staircase and menacingly remarks, 'Yes – the hope that always deludes.'

She then poses her second enigma:

It flickers like a flame, but is not flame. It is sometimes delirious, a feverish, driving force of passion. Inertia makes it languorous and if you lose heart or die, it grows cold. But it flares up if you dream of conquest. You hear its voice with trepidation and it glows like the sunset.

This time, Calàf hesitates and the crowd, now on his side, urge him not to lose heart but to answer, 'for the sake of your life!'

Liù, coming forward anxiously, implores him, 'Answer for the sake of love.'

Calàf then realises the answer and tells Turandot, 'Yes, Princess, when you look at me it rises and falls in my veins. It is Blood.'

Turandot, thinking she has won again, is making her way back to the top of the staircase when he answers but stops and turns back as the Wise Men acknowledge that Calàf is right. Her anger increases as some of the onlookers call to Calàf to 'Take heart, solver of riddles' and she orders the guards to 'Strike down those villains!'

She then comes down the stairs and stands facing Calàf as she puts the third enigma:

Ice that sets you on fire, and is frozen still more by your fire. Pure and dark, if you want to be free it makes you a slave. If it accepts you as a slave, it makes you a King.

Calàf is silent and she taunts him, 'Stranger, you turn pale with fear', and for the moment, baffled, he kneels at her feet. She tells him, 'You know you are lost', then completes the enigma: 'Stranger, what is this ice which gives you fire?'

There is a long silence, then Calàf suddenly springs to his feet and replies, 'My victory now gives you to me. My fire will thaw you – Turandot.'

When the Wise Men have confirmed that 'Turandot' is the correct answer, the crowd applauds Calàf as the victor. Turandot, appalled, begs her father not to let the stranger take her but Altoum replies that his oath is sacred. Still insisting that no man will ever possess her, she then appeals to Calàf – does he want her against her will? He replies that he does not – 'I want you ardent with love' – and he reverses their original roles by making *her* a challenge. If she can discover his name by dawn, she can have him beheaded like the suitors who failed. Turandot agrees but Altoum says that he hopes that when dawn arrives, it will be Calàf who wins this final contest.

Determined that she will beat him, Turandot decrees that nobody in Peking must sleep that night, until the stranger's name is discovered. Calàf is confident that he will win but the people are afraid that Turandot will have them all put to death if she does not find out his name by dawn. Ping, Pang and Pong try to bribe Calàf to leave the city, then Turandot's guards seize Liù and Timur. They have been seen talking to Calàf and the guards suspect that they know his name. Turandot questions Timur, and Liù, fearing for the old man, insists that she is the only one who knows the stranger's name. A crowd of onlookers has gathered and they call for Liù to be tortured to make her speak. Calàf tries to protect her but is seized by the guards.

Tortured, Liù refuses to reveal the stranger's name and when Turandot wonders at her strength, she replies that it comes from her love for him. She makes a prediction that before dawn Turandot will also love him, then, afraid that if she is tortured again she may betray him, she snatches a dagger from one of the guards and stabs herself. She staggers towards Calàf, who is still held by the guards, and dies at his feet. Her face is immediately veiled by Turandot's maidservants, to spare their mistress's feelings. The crowd are moved by Liù's death and murmur that it has been caused by injustice. Fearing that her spirit may return to avenge her, they carry her body reverently away.

Calàf then advances on Turandot, calling her 'Princess of ice and cruelty', and tears the veil from her face. Furious, she tells him that he will not profane her and that she is the Daughter of Heaven, with a spirit far above his. Calàf retorts that her spirit may be above him but her body is beside him and he kisses her passionately. Turandot is not angered by this violation but bewildered – 'What is happening? I am lost' – and finds that for the first time in her life she is weeping.

She then admits to Calàf that she feared him from the first moment that she saw him as his eyes had 'the light of the heroes'. Knowing that she is conquered, she pleads with him to go and to take his mystery with him but Calàf, acknowledging his victory, says that he no longer has a mystery. He tells her his name and says that she can now destroy him. The trumpets then sound to signal the start of the new trial and Calàf, taking Turandot with him, walks confidently away to attend it – but there is no trial. Turandot proclaims that the stranger's name is Love – and, amid great rejoicing from the assembled crowd, she and Calàf embrace.

Puccini composed the music up to the point where Liù's body is carried away by the crowd, leaving Calàf and Turandot together for their final confrontation. Whatever purist objections there may be to the score having been completed by another composer, it must surely be admitted that without the final scenes, most audiences would feel more than a little cheated at not knowing what eventually happened. It could, of course, have been covered in a programme note but that might only have increased the sense of dissatisfaction, with a great many people probably feeling, 'If only we could have seen it!'

It's generally agreed that Puccini produced some of his finest music for *Turandot*, and it was certainly some of his most innovative. As he did in *Madama Butterfly* he gave the opera some appropriate oriental sounds, in this case by using the triangle, gong, xylophone and glockenspiel. In the first act the crowd wait for the moon to rise so that the execution of Turandot's latest suitor can take place, and when it does there is the sad sound of boys singing offstage to a traditional Chinese folk song, 'Moon Lee Wha'. Another, 'Sian Chok', is used for Liù's solo 'Signore, ascolta' ('Listen to me, my Lord') which she sings towards the end of the act when she begs Calàf not to take up Turandot's challenge. This is a fairly short piece but it has been recorded by such distinguished sopranos as the great Maria Callas, although her appearances in the opera were as Turandot.

'Signore, ascolta' begins a magnificent finale to the first act. Liù tells Calàf that Timur will lose a son, while she will lose 'the shadow of a smile' – her devotion to him began, as she says, when 'one day in the palace you smiled at me'. When she ends, 'Liù can endure no more, hear her cry!' Calàf's reply is in the aria 'Non piangere Liù' ('Do not weep, Liù') which becomes an ensemble as Timur, Liù, Ping, Pang and Pong and a chorus all join him. Calàf tells Liù that Timur may soon be alone in the world and tells her not to desert him. She predicts that without him, they will die on the road to exile but Calàf just begs her to make the path easier for Timur. Ping, Pang and Pong join Timur in trying to drag Calàf from the gong but, declaring that 'Glory awaits me there', he strikes it, committing himself to Turandot's challenge.

Ping, Pang and Pong throw up their hands and run off, laughing exasperatedly at the folly of the latest hothead to abandon common sense after a glimpse of Turandot's beauty. Puccini then brings the act to a close, very much as he ended the first act of *Tosca* when he repeatedly thunders out the 'Scarpia' theme, underlining the situation which has built up. Nobody underlines quite like Puccini and at the end of the first act of *Turandot* he does so to perfection. The fate of Turandot's unsuccessful suitors has been shown and by striking the gong Calàf has put himself in danger of following them. Timur and Liù look on, dismayed, but far from showing any trepidation at what he has undertaken, Calàf stands triumphantly, thinking only of the joy that success will bring. The battle is set and, as if in anticipation of a titanic struggle to come, the orchestra reprises the last part of the ensemble, which later becomes the 'Turandot' theme, with ever more menacing repetitions of the last two chords. In the whole of opera there can be no more impressive a climax.

The drama of the first act is renewed in the second, when Turandot puts her riddles to Calàf, but before that there is a scene in which Ping, Pang and Pong discuss the situation and regret the state into which the country has fallen through Turandot's slaughtering of her suitors. Sardonically, they sum up the ceremony of the enigmas as 'Three beats of the gong, three riddles and off with more heads.' They agree that the nation's troubles would be ended by a successful suitor. The scene does nothing to advance the plot but it provides an interval between two highly charged episodes, with the second ushered in by a distant fanfare, telling the three courtiers that the latest contest is about to begin. Resignedly, they trudge off 'to enjoy yet another execution'.

There is a dramatic build-up to the trial scene. When the Wise Men and the three courtiers have taken their places, the Emperor Altoum enters to a chorus of 'May the Emperor live for a thousand years.' When he has seated himself on his throne at the top of the staircase he tells Calàf of 'the terrible oath' which binds him. To each of his three appeals, the last of which is 'Let me die without the burden of your young life', Calàf's reply is the same – 'Son of Heaven, I ask you to let me try my fortune.'

Wearily, Altoum then tells him, 'I leave you to your fate', and a mandarin reads out the conditions of the contest. Turandot's entrance is to a soft, melodic chorus in her praise by offstage children's voices after which, in complete contrast, she sings the dramatic and chilling aria 'In questa reggia' ('In this palace many thousands of years ago, a desperate cry was heard'). The cry was that of her ancestress Lo-u-Ling, and 'has passed down the generations and found refuge in my heart'.

She goes on to tell Calàf that Lo-u-Ling now lives again in her. The empire of that time was conquered and the princess 'dragged away' by a man – 'a stranger like yourself' – and her young voice was stilled. 'I take revenge for that cry, that death,' Turandot warns him. 'No man shall ever possess me. Stranger, do not tempt fortune.'

Most of the aria is sung in a hard, recitative-like manner as Turandot relentlessly states her motivation and her intentions. This gives a greater impact to the ending, when she delivers her final warning – 'The enigmas are three but death is one' – to a new, almost triumphant theme, suggesting that she already senses victory. When Calàf responds with 'No, the enigmas are three, *life is one*', it's to the same theme. He and Turandot then repeat their own versions, simultaneously, competing with each other and the onlookers, excited by this clash of wills, urge Turandot to begin the contest.

For a few moments, she is silent, then looks down at Calàf at the foot of the staircase and immediately begins the first enigma with a menacing 'Listen, stranger.'

The contest provides the dramatic highlight of the act, with Turandot putting her questions with a sense of confidence – and loathing. The tension mounts as Calàf answers the first with the word 'Esperanza' (Hope), which the Wise Men echo several times to confirm that he is correct and then, after some hesitation, he solves the second with the word 'Sangue' (Blood), which is also echoed. The drama reaches its climax when, after kneeling before the triumphant Princess, Calàf suddenly rises to his feet and gives the correct answer, 'Turandot'. The Wise Men repeat her name several times as the beaten Princess stands transfixed on the staircase and the chorus then sing the song of praise to which she entered, but now in honour of Calàf – 'Glory to the victor, may love and life now smile on you.'

Turandot slowly makes her way to the top of the staircase and kneels by Altoum's throne and appeals to him, 'Noble father, don't throw your daughter into the arms of a stranger.' But Altoum's answer is simple: 'My oath is sacred.'

Standing, she looks for sympathy to the crowd and tells Altoum, 'Your daughter is sacred. Don't give me to him like a slave.' Glancing at Calàf, she insists, 'I shall never be yours.'

Altoum again tells her, 'My oath is sacred' and the crowd adds its voice. 'Princess, he won. He offered his life and you are the reward.'

Turandot then appeals to Calàf, 'Would you have me in your arms by force, reluctant, trembling?'

When he has replied that he wants her 'ardent with love', Calàf makes his own challenge – 'You asked me three riddles and I solved them. I shall set you only one.'

As he reminds her that she does not know his name, the orchestra plays the theme of his great aria 'Nessun dorma' ('None shall sleep'), which he sings in the last act. He continues, but not to that theme, to make his challenge, 'Tell me my name by dawn.' Finally, singing to the tune of the aria, he ends his solo, 'And at dawn I shall die.' In the last act, that last phrase becomes, 'At dawn I shall be *victorious*.'

Altoum tells him, 'Heaven hopes that when the sun rises, you will be my son', then exits, followed by Turandot. As they disappear, the crowd again sings the song of praise and the act ends with Calàf standing alone, with Timur and Liù watching him anxiously, as they did in the previous act, after he had struck the gong to accept Turandot's challenge.

Act 3 opens at night, before Altoum's palace. A chorus of tenors repeats Turandot's order that nobody in Peking must sleep that night until the stranger's name has been discovered. Calàf, waiting by the palace, then sings the aria 'None shall sleep' in which he addresses the Princess 'in her cold room, watching the stars which throb with love and hope'.

His secret, he tells her, is hidden within him and nobody shall know his name until he tells it 'on your lips' at daylight, when 'My kiss shall make you mine.'

A distant chorus of Turandot's subjects is heard, predicting that they will all die because of him, but Calàf completes the aria, 'Let the night depart, the stars set. At dawn I shall be victorious', repeating the final word 'vinceró' twice, each time more impressively. Then, however, Ping, Pang and Pong appear and tell him to lower his eyes from the stars, as their lives are in his hands. 'Take these,' they urge him, bringing in some beautiful, half-naked girls. Calàf rejects them, and also the jewels and various other riches which they offer him.

When he implores the dawn to hurry and 'end this nightmare' the three men tell him that he does not know what the cruel Princess might do to him, or what tortures have been invented in China. They and the crowd urge him to save them by revealing his name and then Timur and Liù are dragged in. Turandot, believing Liù's claim that she is the only one who knows the stranger's name, orders her torture. When she queries the girl's strength in the face of this torture, Liù's answer is in her aria, 'Tanto amore segreto' ('My secret, unspoken love is so great that these tortures seem sweet to me because I offer them as a gift to my master'), and she tells Turandot, 'I give you to him and I lose everything, even my impossible hopes. Let me suffer every torment as the supreme offering of my love.'

Before she stabs herself to avoid further torture which might force her to betray Calàf, Liù has a final, short aria, 'Tue che di gel sei cinta' ('You who are girded in ice'), the words of which were actually written by Puccini. Strangely reversing his usual practice, he composed the music for the aria before he received the verse from his librettists, then wrote the words to it. When they read them, Adami and Simoni felt that they could not produce anything better and so, in what was almost his final contribution to his last opera, Puccini left something which was entirely his own. The words were:

> You who are girded in ice,
> Conquered by such fire,
> You will love him too.
> I'll close my tired eyes before dawn,
> So that he may conquer again.
> I'll never see him again.

After Puccini's funeral march to which the body of Liù is carried away, Alfano composed the score, including Turandot's aria 'Del primo pianto' ('Of my first tear'), which she sings after Calàf, almost in desperation, has kissed her and she finds herself weeping. The aria is followed by the duet between Calàf and Turandot, which Puccini had wanted to be a 'great duet'. Turandot has a final solo in which she tells the onlookers that 'Il suo nome è Amor' ('His name is Love') and the finale is to Puccini's own theme of 'Nessun dorma' – confirming that as he predicted when he challenged Turandot, at dawn Calàf is victorious.

Turandot provides scope for a lot of speculation. Puccini's sad poem, stating that he would be happy to rest when death came to find him and his plea to Toscanini, 'Don't let my *Turandot* die', suggest strongly that he knew death was not far off – which might have been a realisation of the possible seriousness of his condition rather than some instinct of fate. Several authors have seen the similarity between Turandot driving Liù to her death and Elvira hounding Doria Manfredi to suicide. He was non-committal when Simoni first suggested *Turandot* as a theme but within a few days seemed totally committed to the idea. Did he, having examined the story, suddenly see a way expiating some guilt that he still felt over the death of Doria?

We may also speculate over what his reaction to Alfano's ending to the opera might have been but it's unlikely that it would have been too far from what would have been his own score. He had, after all, seen the verses for the final duet before he left for Brussels and expressed general satisfaction, and Alfano did use his notes to complete the score. What might have disappointed him was that he wrote the part of Liù for his favourite soprano Gilda dalla Rizza but she was unable to sing it at the premiere – although Maria Zamboni, who was cast in the role on that occasion, was a very able substitute.

Puccini's death made the premiere an emotional event and consequently it was almost certain that *Turandot* would be well received by the audience and the press – and it was particularly sad that, having finally achieved the successful premiere at La Scala that had previously eluded him, he was not there to see it. The lasting popularity of the opera shows, however, this was not due only to respect and sentiment. In *Turandot* Puccini combined the skill and experience of a truly great artist and if, as it is often claimed, it was the last great Italian opera to be produced, he could have wished for no greater honour to provide the final chapter to such a wonderful story.

Principal Characters

ALCINDORO   *La Bohème*   Bass
An elderly state councillor who is Musetta's admirer. She abandons him at the Café Momus, where she meets up again with Marcello, her real love.

ALTOUM   *Turandot*   Tenor
Emperor and Turandot's father. When Calàf solves Turandot's enigmas, he refuses to go back on his oath to allow her successful challenger to marry her.

SISTER ANGELICA   *Suor Angelica*   Soprano
Sent to a convent when she has an illegitimate child. Visited by her aunt, the Princess, who wants her to renounce her inheritance. Commits suicide when the aunt tells her that the child has died.

ANGELOTTI   *Tosca*   Bass
Escaped political prisoner who hides in the church where the artist Cavaradossi is painting a picture of Mary Magdalene. Later commits suicide to avoid being recaptured by Scarpia, the Chief of Police.

ANNA WULF   *Le Villi*   Soprano
Daughter of the forester Guglielmo and betrothed to Roberto. Dies when he deserts her and, as one of the Villi, takes her revenge on him.

ASHBY   *La Fanciulla del West*   Bass
Wells Fargo agent in pursuit of Ramerrez and his Mexican gang.

BENOIT   *La Bohème*   Bass
Landlord of the four Bohemians, who often tries unsuccessfully to collect the rent they owe him.

BILLY JACKRABBIT   *La Fanciulla del West*   Bass
Red Indian whose squaw, Wowkle, is Minnie's servant.

THE BONZE   *Madama Butterfly*   Bass
Butterfly's uncle and a Bhuddist priest who denounces her for forsaking her traditional gods when she marries Pinkerton.

CALÀF   *Turandot*   Tenor
The unknown prince who accepts Turandot's challenge and solves her enigmas.

CASTRO   *La Fanciulla del West*   Bass
A 'greaser' (Mexican) in Ramerrez's gang. Captured by the Wells Fargo agent Ashby, and brought in when Johnson (Ramerrez) is in the saloon. Does not identify Johnson but leads Ashby and the miners on a false trail in pursuit of him.

CAVARADOSSI   *Tosca*   Tenor
An artist who is in love with Tosca. Arrested and tortured by Scarpia, the Chief of Police, he is finally killed in what is supposed to be a fake execution.

CIO-CIO SAN (BUTTERFLY) *Madama Butterfly*   Soprano
Young former geisha who marries the American navy lieutenant Pinkerton but commits hara-kiri when he returns with an American wife to take their son from her.

COLLINE *La Bohème* Bass
One of the bohemians, a philosopher. In the final act, pawns his old coat to buy medicine for the dying Mimi.

DES GRIEUX *Manon Lescaut* Tenor
Student who meets Manon when she is on her way to a convent and falls in love with her. Follows her to America when she is deported and dies with her in the desert when he thinks he has killed a man in a duel over her.

EDGAR *Edgar* Tenor
Leaves his lover Fidelia for the exotic gypsy Tigrana, regrets his actions and finally regains Fidelia, only to see her murdered by Tigrana.

EDMONDO *Manon Lescaut* Tenor
Fellow student with Des Grieux and helps him to escape with Manon when the wealthy Geronte has designs on her.

FIDELIA *Edgar* Soprano
Lover of Edgar and remains faithful to him when he has left her for Tigrana. Edgar finally declares his love for her, whereupon she is killed by Tigrana.

FLORIA TOSCA *Tosca* Soprano
Famous singer and lover of Cavaradossi. Agrees to give herself to Scarpia if he will spare Cavaradossi's life when he has been arrested. Stabs Scarpia when he has signed a release for them but when Cavaradossi is killed, in what is supposed to be a fake execution, she throws herself from the battlements as Scarpia's men come to arrest her.

FRANK *Edgar* Baritone
Brother of Fidelia, who shares Edgar's infatuation with Tigrana and fights him when he is about to leave their village with her.

GERONTE DE RAVOIR — *Manon Lescaut* — Bass
Rich Treasurer General who lures Manon away from Des Grieux but has her arrested as an immoral woman when she tires of him and plans to go off with Des Grieux.

GHERARDO — *Gianni Schicchi* — Tenor
Cousin of the deceased Buoso Donati, and present when the relations ask Gianni Schicchi to help them when it is learned that Buoso has left none of his most valuable possessions to the family.

GIANNI SCHICCHI — *Gianni Schicchi* — Baritone
Called in by the Donati family when they find that their rich relation Buoso has left his most valuable possessions to the monks. Offended by their attitude to him, he is about to withdraw but his daughter Lauretta begs him to come back as her lover Rinuccio, a member of the Donati family, needs an inheritance to marry her. Schicchi relents, but tricks the family by faking a will for Buoso that leaves the most valuable assets to himself.

GIORGETTA — *Il Tabarro* — Soprano
Michele's wife who is having an affair with Luigi, the stevedore, who is murdered by Michele.

GORO — *Madama Butterfly* — Tenor
Marriage broker who arranges Butterfly's marriage to Pinkerton and later tries to persuade her to accept Prince Yamadori when Pinkerton has married an American girl.

GUALTIERO — *Edgar* — Bass
Father of Fidelia and Frank.

GUGLIELMO WULF — *Le Villi* — Baritone
Father of Anna, who invokes the Villi when Roberto has deserted her and she dies of a broken heart.

JOHNSON   *La Fanciulla del West*   Tenor

Forced into a life of crime as the bandit leader Ramerrez. Falls in love with Minnie, who saves him from the sheriff Rance and they go off together to start a new life.

KATE   *Madama Butterfly*   Mezzo-Soprano

Marries Pinkerton and returns to Nagasaki with him, agreeing to adopt the son that has been born to him and Butterfly.

LAURETTA   *Gianni Schicchi*   Soprano

Daughter of Gianni Schicchi, who persuades him to help the Donati family to benefit from Buoso's will, so that they will allow Rinuccio, their relation, to marry her.

LISETTE   *La Rondine*   Soprano

Magda's maid, who makes an unsuccessful attempt at a stage career. When she returns to Magda and takes up her old duties it is an object lesson to her mistress, who has just ended a relationship in which her partner did not know of her real age and past life – they are both happier when they are not trying to be something that they are not.

LIÚ   *Turandot*   Soprano

Slave girl who remains faithful to the blind Timur when he is deposed as king of Tartary. Loves his son Calàf and kills herself for fear that she will reveal his name when Turandot has her tortured.

LUIGI   *Il Tabarro*   Tenor

Stevedore who works for Michele, the barge owner, and has an affair with his wife Giorgetta. Comes onto the barge at night when he sees what he believes to be a signal from Giorgetta and is caught by Michele, who strangles him.

MAGDA DE CIVRY   *La Rondine*   Soprano
Mistress of Rambaldo Fernandez who seeks happiness with the
young Ruggero Lastouc, by pretending to be much younger than she
is. Finally leaves him when she realises that the pretence cannot be
sustained.

MANON LESCAUT   *Manon Lescaut*   Soprano
Beautiful but rather venal eponymous heroine who loves the student
Des Greux but brings about her own downfall by allowing herself to
be lured away from him by a rich man.

MARCELLO   *La Bohème*   Baritone
A painter, one of the Bohemians and a close friend of Rodolfo. A
kindly man, his on/off relationship with the singer Musetta gives
some comic relief in a sad story.

MICHELE   *Il Tabarro*   Baritone
Barge owner whose wife Giorgetta is only half his age and is having
an affair with the stevedore Luigi. When he lights his pipe one night
Luigi sees the flame and believes it to be a signal from Giorgetta.
Michele catches him when he comes onto the barge and, after forcing
him to confess the affair, he strangles him.

MIMI   *La Bohème*   Soprano
Tragic heroine of Puccini's most popular opera. Meets and quickly
falls in love with the hero, Rodolfo. They part because of his apparent
jealousy – he is actually afraid that he is too poor to help her overcome
the consumption from which she is dying and wants her to find a
wealthier companion – but she returns to him just before she dies.

MINNIE   *La Fanciulla del West*   Soprano
Runs the Polka saloon in California, gives Bible readings to the
miners and looks after their old for them. Meets Johnson, not
knowing that he is Ramerrez the bandit, and falls in love with him.

MUSETTA   *La Bohème*   Soprano
A singer who has a volatile relationship with the painter Marcello.
At the end of the opera she sells her earrings to buy medicine for the
dying Mimi.

NELLA   *Gianni Schicchi*   Soprano
Wife of Buoso's nephew Gherardo. With the other women, helps
Schicchi to change into Buoso's clothes so that he can pose as him
and dictate a new will to the notary.

NICK   *La Fanciulla del West*   Tenor
Minnie's bartender in the Polka saloon. When he goes to Minnie's
cabin with a posse hunting Johnson, he realises that she is hiding the
bandit there, but out of loyalty to her he does not say so. When the
miners are about to hang Johnson, he rides off to tell Minnie so that
she can save him.

PANG   *Turandot*   Tenor
Major domo in the palace of the Emperor Altoum, father of
Turandot. With Ping and Pong he forms a semi-comic trio of
courtiers who regret the state of the country as Turandot is executing
her unsuccessful suitors.

PARPIGNOL   *La Bohème*   Tenor
A toy vendor who appears by the Café Momus when the Bohemians
are having a meal there on Christmas Eve.

PING   *Turandot*   Baritone
Altoum's Lord Chancellor. He and his two companions try to
dissuade Calàf from taking up Turandot's challenge.

PINKERTON   *Madama Butterfly*   Tenor
Lieutenant in the US Navy who marries Butterfly but does not take
the match seriously. Returns to Nagasaki with an American wife

to take the son that has been born to him and Butterfly, prompting Butterfly's suicide.

| PONG | *Turandot* | Tenor |

Chief chef in Altoum's palace. Companion of Ping and Pang.

| THE PRINCESS | *Sua Angelica* | Contralto |

Angelica's aunt, who tells her of the death of her child, after which Angelica commits suicide.

| PRUNIER | *La Rondine* | Tenor |

A poet who, trying his hand at palmistry, predicts that Magda will 'go south like the Swallow [La Rondine]' in search of happiness. Helps Magda's maid Lisette in her unsuccessful attempt at a stage career.

| RAMBALDO FERNANDEZ | *La Rondine* | Baritone |

Wealthy man who accepts it with dignity when his mistress, Magda de Civry, leaves him for a younger man and readily takes her back when her adventure ends.

| JACK RANCE | *La Fanciulla del West* | Baritone |

The sheriff who loves Minnie and resents it when she is attracted to Johnson. When he finds that Johnson is really Ramerrez the bandit and captures him, he tries to hang him but the miners, loyal to Minnie, intervene.

| RINUCCIO | *Gianni Schicchi* | Tenor |

The nephew of Zita, the deceased Buoso's cousin. Wants to marry Gianni Schicchi's daughter Lauretta but needs the money from Buoso's will so that the family cannot prevent it. Persuades them to let Schicchi help them when they find that Buoso has left most his most valuable assets to the local monks.

ROBERTO   *Le Villi*   Tenor

Betrothed to Anna Wulf but does not return to her when he goes away to collect an inheritance. He comes back after she has died of a broken heart and, now as one of the Villi, she takes her revenge by forcing him to dance with her until he dies of exhaustion.

RODOLFO   *La Bohème*   Tenor

A poet and one of the Bohemians. Falls in love with the consumptive Mimi but drives her away by pretending to be jealous because he is too poor to help her in her fragile state. When she is dying, she comes back to him so that they can spend her last moments together.

RUGGERO LASTOUC   *La Rondine*   Tenor

A young man from the country, the son of a friend of Rambaldo. When he comes to Rambaldo's house on his first visit to Paris, Rambaldo's mistress Magda tells him to go to a nearby restaurant, then meets him there, disguised as a grisette. Ruggero falls in love with her, believing her to be much younger and more innocent than she is. They live together for a while but when he talks of marrying her, Magda realises that their association must end and goes back to Rambaldo.

SACRISTAN   *Tosca*   Bass

Is in the church where the artist Cavaradossi is painting a portrait of Mary Magdalene. Disapproves when he realises that Cavaradossi has given the portrait of a young woman who comes there to pray.

SCARPIA   *Tosca*   Baritone

Corrupt Sicilian Chief of Police who lusts after Tosca. When he has arrested her lover Cavaradossi, he bargains with her, telling her that he will arrange a fake execution after which they can escape, if she will submit to him. Tosca agrees but stabs him when he has signed the safe passage for him. Too late, she finds that the execution was real.

SCHAUNARD   *La Bohème*   Baritone

A musician and one of the Bohemians. When Mimi is dying he encourages his friend Colline to pawn his old coat to buy medicine for her.

SHARPLESS   *Madama Butterfly*   Baritone

US Consul who is concerned that Pinkerton is not taking his marriage to Butterfly seriously. When he knows that Pinkerton has married an American girl, he does his best to persuade her to marry Prince Yamadori, thinking that it will be in her best interests.

SID   *La Fanciulla del West*   Baritone

A miner caught cheating at cards by Rance, the sheriff, who pins two cards to his jacket to show that he is a cheat.

SONORA   *La Fanciulla del West*   Baritone

A miner who loves Minnie but, when he see that she loves Johnson, helps her to save him from being hanged.

SPOLETTA   *Tosca*   Tenor

Right-hand man of Scarpia, the corrupt Chief of Police, who faithfully carries out the order that means that the 'fake' execution of Cavaradossi will actually be real.

SUZUKI   *Madama Butterfly*   Mezzo-Soprano

Butterfly's faithful maid and companion, who turns on Goro, the marriage broker, when he spreads false stories about her mistress. She does her best to stop Butterfly from committing suicide.

TIGRANA   *Edgar*   Mezzo-Soprano

Beautiful gypsy girl who elopes with Edgar and is later bribed to denounce him when she has been tricked into believing that he is dead. When he reveals that he is still alive and declares his love for Fidelia, she stabs her.

TIMUR   *Turandot*   Bass

Blind deposed king of Tartary who travels with the faithful slave girl Liù and meets up with his son Calàf in Peking, and unsuccessfully tries to dissuade him from taking up Turandot's challenge.

TURANDOT   *Turandot*   Soprano

Beautiful princess, daughter of the Emperor Altoum, who challenges her suitors to solve her three enigmas – if they do, they can marry her; but if they fail, they are executed. Eventually beaten by the unknown prince Calàf.

JAKE WALLACE   *La Fanciulla del West*   Baritone

Town minstrel who, in the first act, leads a chorus in a song about the hardships of the mining life.

WOWKLE   *La Fanciulla del West*   Mezzo-Soprano

Minnie's servant and squaw of Billy Jackrabbit.

PRINCE YAMADORI   *Madama Butterfly*   Tenor

Introduced to Butterfly by Goro, the marriage broker, when Pinkerton has written to Sharpless, the Consul, informing him that he now has an American wife.

ZITA   *Gianni Schicchi*   Contralto

Also called 'La Vecchia' (The Old Woman), she is the cousin of the deceased Buoso Donati and aunt of Rinuccio, who is in love with Gianni Schicchi's daughter Lauretta. She disapproves of Schicchi but agrees to let him help the family by forging a new will for Buoso.

Performers

ADAMI, Giuseppe (1878–1946)
Librettist, playwright and screenwriter born in Verona. Introduced to Puccini by Ricordi, he failed to interest him in another project but wrote the libretti for *La Rondine* and *Il Tabarro* and later, with Simoni, *Turandot*. His biography of Puccini, *Il Romanzo della vita di Giacomo Puccini*, was published in Milan in 1935.

ALFANO, Franco (1875–1954)
Completed the score of *Turandot* after Puccini's death, using sketches that the composer had made. Born at Posillipo, Naples, he was well known in Italy as a composer in his own right. As well as operas, he wrote groups of songs and orchestral works.

AMATO, Pasquale (1878–1942)
Baritone who created the role of Jack Rance in *La Fanciulla del West*. A native of Naples, he sang in many leading roles at La Scala, Milan, under Toscanini. In 1904 he sang with Caruso in *Carmen* at Covent Garden but his main successes were in New York, where he was a regular member of the Metropolitan Opera Company from 1908 to 1921. He was still living in New York, in Jackson's Heights, when he died.

CAMPANINI, Cleofonte (1860–1919)
Conducted the disastrous first performance of *Madama Butterfly* in 1904. Born at Parma, where he was sent to study the violin at the

Regia Scuola di Musica. He was expelled for lack of discipline but continued his musical career and was soon successful, deputising as conductor for the well-known Franco Faccio. His career as an operatic conductor began with a performance of *Carmen* at Parma in 1882. He spent the latter part of his life in the USA and died in Chicago, where he had been conductor for the Chicago Opera Association.

CAPONETTI, Regina
Soprano. Puccini's first heroine, as she sang the part of Anna Wulf in *Le Villi* at the premiere in Turin, 1884. That was her only notable achievement and little else about her is known.

CARUSO, Enrico (1873–1921)
World-famous tenor – one of the greatest of all time – who sang most of the better known Puccini roles but created only that of Dick Johnson (Ramerrez) in *La Fanciulla del West* in 1910. He had great natural talent but struggled initially, through lack of formal training. His first real success was in *La Giaconda* at Palermo. He was born and died in Naples, but refused to sing there again after his performance in *L'Elisir Amore* was badly received.

CATTANEO, Aurelia (1864–91)
Soprano who created the role of Fidelia in *Edgar*. She was the first Italian soprano to sing Isolde, but her brilliant career came to a sad and premature end when she died giving birth.

CIVINNI, Guelfo (1873–1954)
Librettist, with Zangarini, for *La Fanciulla del West*. Born in Livorno, he was a journalist and foreign correspondent for several major newspapers and a poet, novelist and travel writer.

CREMONINI, Giuseppe (1885–1939)
Tenor who sang both Luigi in *Il Tabarro* and Rinuccio in *Gianni Schicchi* at the first performance of *Il Trittico* in 1918. Born at

Paternò, he made his debut as Manrico in *Il Trovatore* – not an easy part for a debut – at Palermo in 1910. Handsome and with an attractive voice, he was ideal for the romantic and verismo roles which were fashionable during his career. He had his last great success in 1924, in Meybeer's *L'Africaine* and spent the next four years teaching. Among the singers he taught was the world-famous baritone Tito Gobbi.

DALLA RIZZA, Gilda (1892–1975)
Born in Verona, a distinguished soprano who created the role of Magda in *La Rondine*, which Puccini wrote for her. She was not first Minnie in *La Fanciulla del West* but when she played in it, Puccini remarked, 'At last I've seen my Fanciulla.' He also wrote the part of Liù in *Turandot* for her but it was sung by Maria Zamboni. When *Il Trittico* had its first Italian performance in Rome in 1919, she sang both Angelica and Lauretta with great success but was not so well received in those parts at Covent Garden in 1921. Greatly admired by Toscanini, she had a repertoire of fifty-eight roles, thirteen of which she created.

D'ANDRADE, Antonio (1854–1942)
Born in Portugal, he went to Italy to further his career and was Puccini's first hero, as he sang the tenor role of Roberto in *Le Villi* in 1884. He retired from singing at quite an early age when he became deaf. He was less successful than his brother Francisco, who was a baritone.

DARCLÉE, Hariclea (1860–1939)
Romanian soprano, who created the role of Tosca. She had a beautiful voice and a wide repertoire but could not overcome a certain coldness in her own character which made her interpretations less convincing than those of other sopranos of the period. Impoverished in her later years, she lived for a while in the Verdi Home in Milan, but died in her native Bucharest.

DE LUCA, Giuseppe (1876–1950)
Created the baritone roles of Sharpless in *Madama Butterfly* and *Gianni Schicchi*. His voice was less powerful than those of some of his contemporaries but his expertise enabled him to continue singing to a greater age. He sang Rigoletto, one of his favourite roles, at the Metropolitan Opera House, New York, when he was sixty-three, and gave a farewell concert there at the age of seventy. He died in New York three years later.

DE MARCHI, Emilio (1861–1917)
Tenor who created the role of Cavaradossi in *Tosca*, and was chosen for the part, much coveted at the time, by Puccini himself. He sang the part in London and later in New York, where he was also very successful in the role of Radames in *Aida*. He died in Milan, where he made his debut, at the age of thirty, at La Scala.

DESTINN, Emmy (Kitti Destinova) (1878–1950)
Created the role of Minnie in *Fanciulla del West* in 1910. Czechoslovakian soprano, born in Prague. A regular at the Metropolitan Opera House, New York, 1908–16, she also played the lead role at the London premiere of *Madame Butterfly*, with Caruso as Pinkerton. She was noted for her acting as well as her singing and played many parts, including Carmen, Santuzza in *Cavalleria Rusticana* – her debut role in 1898 – and Aida. She sang in many different countries but never lost touch with her native Czechoslovakia, where she died.

DIDUR, Adamo (1874–1946)
Bass who created the roles of Ashby in *Fanciulla del West* and Talpa in *Il Tabarro*. Born Wola Sekowa in Poland in 1874. A first-class actor who sang in South America and London – where he appeared as Colline in *La Bohème* in 1905 – he then had a long career in the USA after he was engaged for the Manhattan Opera in 1907, and later at the Metropolitan from 1908 to 1933. He created the role of Boris Godunov in 1913. He returned to Poland after he retired and died in Katowice.

EASTON, Florence (1884–1936)
Soprano who created the role of Lauretta in *Gianni Schicchi*. Born in Middlesbrough, she was one of the few English sopranos to succeed in Grand Opera but made relatively few appearances at Covent Garden. One of these was as Butterfly in 1909 and when *Turandot* was first performed there in 1927 she made three appearances in the title role, taking over from another soprano, Bianca Scacciati, after the opening night. Her versatility is shown by the fact that she had a repertoire of thirty-five roles and sang parts as different as Brünhilde and Carmen. She gave an acclaimed performance as Brünhilde, at the age of fifty-two, in 1936. She spent much of her time in the USA, having married an American tenor, Francis MacLennan, and died in New York.

FACCIO, Franco (1840–91)
Conducted Puccini's *Capricio Sinfonico*, the composer's 'finishing piece' when he completed his studies at the Milan Conservatoire and at the premiere of *Edgar* in 1889. He is said to have been love with Romilda Pantaleoni, who played Tigrana in *Edgar*. Born in Verona, he also composed and was a lifelong friend of Verdi's librettist Arrigo Boito. He had a varied and strenuous career, which may have led to his early death of general paralysis, in an asylum in Monza.

FARRAR, Geraldine (1882–1967)
American soprano, born in Melrose, Massachusetts, in 1882. She created the role of Sister Angelica and was one of the leading singers with the Metropolitan Opera in New York for sixteen years from 1906. Two of her most popular roles were Butterfly and Carmen. She died in Ridgefield, Connecticut.

FERRANI, Cesira (1863–1943)
Soprano who first sang the roles of Manon Lescaut and Mimi but did not have a particularly long or successful career. She made her debut in Turin in 1887 as Micaëla in *Carmen*, originated the two Puccini

roles in 1893 and 1896 but retired at the comparatively early age of thirty-seven in 1900.

FERRARIS, Ines Maria (1882–1971)

Practically forgotten soprano who sang the part of Lisette at the premiere of *La Rondine*, nine years after she made her debut at Bologna. Very popular in South America, she had a wide repertoire, including roles by Verdi and Richard Strauss.

FLETA, Miguel (1893–1938)

Spanish tenor, born in Albalate de Cinca, who created the role of Calàf in *Turandot*. He made his debut in 1919 in Trieste in *Francesca da Rimini* and then appeared in Vienna, Rome, Monte Carlo, Madrid and Buenos Aires in *Rigoletto*, *Aida*, *Tosca* and his most successful role, Don José in *Carmen*. His failure to look after his voice resulted in a shortened career and he returned to Spain, where he died in La Caruña.

FONTANA, Ferdinando (1850–1919)

Librettist for *Le Villi* and *Edgar*, who was recommended to Puccini by Ponchielli. Also a journalist, he once said that he found writing libretti 'tedious' – probably as a ploy to obtain a better fee. He helped Puccini to have *Le Villi* performed after it was unplaced in the Sonzogno Prize competition. He also suggested *Edgar* to Puccini as suitable for an opera but his libretto was not a good one and the opera failed.

FORZANO, Giovacchino (1883–1970)

Playwright and stage director who wrote the libretti for *Suor Angelica* – which he based on his own one-act play – and *Gianni Schicchi*. Born at Borgo San Lorenzo, he trained as a baritone and often sang in provincial productions in Italy, then wrote libretti for Mascagni, Wolf-Ferrari, Leoncavallo and Giordano. He produced the premieres of *Turandot* and Boito's *Nerone*, and a number of other operas in several European countries.

GABRIELESCO, Gregorio
Romanian tenor who originated the title role in *Edgar* in 1889, the
year in which he had his only season at La Scala. His most successful
role was Enzo in *La Giaconda*.

GIACONIA, Giuseppina
Mezzo-soprano who created the role of Suzuki in *Madama Butterfly*
and sang the part again at the successful second performance in
Brescia.

GIACOSA, Giuseppe (1847–1906)
Librettist for *Manon Lescaut*, *La Bohème*, *Tosca* and *Madama
Butterfly*. He was already established as a playwright, author and
most importantly a poet when the publisher Ricordi asked him for
advice on *Manon Lescaut* after the composer had been dissatisfied
first with the work of Leoncavallo, and then of Praga and Oliva. He
suggested that Ricordi should approach Luigi Illica, but later became
involved and then continued to collaborate with Illica on the other
three operas. His death also ended Puccini's association with Illica,
who the composer did not consider to be adequate to complete a
libretto unaided.

GILLY, Dinh (1877–1940)
French tenor, born in Algiers, who created the role of Sonora in
Fanciulla del West and sang the baritone part of Jack Rance in the
British premiere. He made his debut as Silvio in *Pagliacci* at the
Paris Opéra in 1903 and was with the Metropolitan Opera, New
York, 1909–14. He was an excellent linguist and a fine actor. With
his English wife Edith Furmedge he opened a school for singers in
London, where he remained until his death.

GIRALDONI, Eugenio (1871–1924)
Baritone – Italian but born in Marseilles – who created the role
of Scarpia in *Tosca*. Widely travelled, as after making his debut as

Escamillo in *Carmen* in Barcelona in 1891, he also sang in Moscow, Odessa and Kiev, and was in Helsinki when he died. He was not regarded as one of the outstanding baritones of his day but had a good stage manner, which would have been necessary in his playing of Scarpia.

GORGA, Evan (1866–1958)

Born Evangelist Gennaro Gorga in Broccostella, east of Rome, he was the first Rodolfo in *La Bohème* and sang the part of Marcello in Leoncavallo's version of the opera in 1897. He received excellent reviews when he sang the part of Rodolfo again in January 1899 at the Teatro Drammatico in Verona, but it was his last performance. Nobody knows why he gave up a successful career at the age of thirty-four. Puccini had to transpose the part of Rodolfo for him at the first performance and commented that he did not think he would 'last'.

ILLICA, Luigi (1857–1919)

Librettist who, with Giuseppe Giacosa, came to Puccini's during the writing of *Manon Lescaut*. He and Giacosa went on to write the libretti of *La Bohème*, *Tosca* and *Madama Butterfly*. He wrote libretti for many other composers, including Catalani, Mascagni and Giordarno. He led a colourful life – it's sometimes said that it resembled his libretti – and was always photographed with his head slightly turned after he lost his right ear in a duel over a woman.

JERITZA, Maria (1887–1982)

A Czechoslovakian soprano, born in Brno, who never originated a Puccini role but was said to be his favourite Tosca. She once caused a sensation by singing the aria 'Vissi d'arte, vissi d'amore' lying prone on the floor – something which, as far as is known, no other soprano has attempted. She was also a celebrated Turandot and sang a number of roles, including various Wagner heroines.

KRUSCENISKI or KRUSHELNYTSKA, Salomea (1872–1952)
Soprano who sang Cio-Cio San in the revised version of *Madama Butterfly* which was put on at Brescia after the disastrous premiere at Milan. She was the only change in the principals, taking over from Rosina Storchio, who was then singing the same role in a production in Buenos Aires, conducted by Toscanini. Born in the Ukraine, she was a woman of great beauty and subtle performance – her interpretations of such roles as Aida and Salome were highly individual. Died in L'vov, Ukraine, where in 1892 she made her highly successful debut.

LEONCAVALLO, Ruggero (1857–1919)
Composer and librettist, born in Naples, remembered mainly for his opera *Pagliacci*, but was involved with the libretto for *Manon Lescaut* until Puccini decided that their ideas were incompatible and asked Ricordi to remove him. He was in dispute with Puccini over who had the greater claim on *La Bohème* and produced his own version which, until Puccini's became well known, was the more successful. He composed a number of operas and travelled widely to promote them but never again matched the success of *Pagliacci*.

MARINUZZI, Gino (1882–1945)
Conductor at the premiere of *La Rondine*. Born at Palermo in Sicily, he was also a composer and wrote three operas, a ballet based on the Pinocchio story, chamber music and a symphony. Well known for his interpretations of Wagner, as well as Italian operas, he had seasons as Chief Conductor at Rome and Covent Garden. Died in Milan, only a year after he had become a director of La Scala.

MASCAGNI, Pietro (1863–1945)
Remembered chiefly as the composer of *Cavalleria Rusticana*. He became a friend of Puccini when they shared lodgings as fellow students at the Milan Conservatoire and played the double bass at the first performance of *Le Villi*. He delivered an oration at Puccini's funeral in 1924.

MAZZARZA, Michele

Bass who was the first Colline in *La Bohème*, but did not have a particularly successful career.

MONTESANTO, Luigi (1887–1954)

Sicilian born baritone who created the role of Michele in *Il Tabarro*. Born in Palermo, where he made his operatic debut in 1909, as Escamillo in *Carmen*. He appeared in New York, where *Il Tabarro* was first performed, and Chicago, as well as most of the leading opera houses in Italy, where his roles included Scarpia in *Tosca*. He retired in 1940, when he settled in Milan and became a teacher. His pupils included the tenor Giuseppe di Stephano, who often appeared with Maria Callas. He remained in Milan until his death.

MORANZONI, Roberto (1880–1959)

Conducted the premiere of *Il Trittico*. Born in Bari, he showed early promise as a musician and, like Puccini, studied with Mascagni. His debut as a conductor was at the Teatro Costanzi, Rome, in 1901, where *Tosca* had had its premiere the previous year. It was during the second of his seven seasons as conductor with the Metropolitan, New York, that *Il Trittico* was premiered there in 1918. He was later with the Chicago Opera but returned to Italy and died in Milan in 1959.

MUGNONE, Leopoldo (1858–1941)

Resident conductor at the Teatro Costanzi in Rome, where *Tosca* had its first performance in 1900. Puccini had also wanted him to conduct the premiere of *La Bohème* but was more than satisfied with Toscanini's interpretation. Mugnone, also noted as a composer, once fell out with Puccini over the direction of a production of *Madama Butterfly* in Rome in 1909, but later, when good relations had been restored, he introduced *La Rondine* in Italy, soon after the Monte Carlo premiere. His interpretations of *Otello* and *Falstaff* were highly regarded by the librettist of those operas, Arrigo Boito.

MUZIO, Claudia (1889–1936)
Soprano who originated the role of Giorgetta in *Il Tabarro* and also
that of Madalena in *Rigoletto*. Her best roles were thought to be
Desdemona in *Otello* and the two Puccini leads Tosca and Mimi,
which she sang with Caruso in 1914. This was during a very successful
season at Covent Garden, where her father had been a stage director.
It was as Tosca that she made her successful debut at the Metropolitan
Opera in New York in 1916, and she sang there for seven consecutive
seasons. She was noted for the sweetness of her voice and her ability
to extract pathos and drama from her various roles.

NESSI, Giuseppe (1887–1961)
Tenor who played Pong at the premiere of *Turandot* and also at the
first performance at Covent Garden, where he appeared regularly
from 1927 to 1937. He sang in London with the La Scala company
at the advanced age of sixty-three.

OLIVA, Domenico (1860–1917)
One of the original librettists for *Manon Lescaut*, he was chosen by
Marco Praga as his collaborator as he was a poet. He left to complete
the libretto when Praga gave up, but also found it difficult to cope
with Puccini's frequent changes of mind and therefore withdrew. He
had a very varied career as a writer, journalist, critic, lawyer and
politician.

PANIZZA, Achille
Thought to have been the conductor at the premiere of *Le Villi*, but
some experts believe that it was one of his two brothers. Argentinian
with Italian ancestry. His son Ettore, also a conductor, had a much
more successful career.

PANTALEONI, Romilda (1847–1917)
Soprano who originated the part of Tigrana in *Edgar* – although
it was a mezzo role. Born at Udine, she was a brilliant actress and

should have found great scope for her talent as Tigrana but disliked the part, finding the character unsympathetic. Among her most successful interpretations were Aida and La Giaconda, but her greatest achievements were to create the roles of Desdemona in Verdi's *Otello* and Santuzza in *Cavalleria Rusticana*.

PASINI, Camilla (1875–1935)
Soprano who played Musetta at the premiere of *La Bohème*. Also sang the parts of Mimi and Puccini's Manon Lescaut.

PERINI, Flora (1887–1975)
Mezzo-soprano who created the role of the Principessa in *Suor Angelica* – which was actually written for a contralto. Born in Rome, she made her debut at La Scala when she was twenty-one. She first appeared at the Metropolitan in *Cavalleria Rusticana* in 1915, and remained in New York until 1924. After a season with the Chicago Opera she returned to Rome in 1925, and died there fifty years later. After her return she sang mainly at the Teatro Constanzi.

PINI CORSI, Antonio (1858–1918)
Baritone, Italian but born in Dalmatia, who created the role of Schaunard in *La Bohème*. After his debut in 1878 he spent a number of years playing mainly comic roles in operas by Rossini and Donizetti, then made his first appearance at La Scala in the title role of *Rigoletto*. Between 1909 and 1914 he appeared regularly at the Metropolitan, New York, and it was there in 1910 that he created the role of the miner Happy in *La Fanciulla del West*. He was still in good voice in 1917, only a year before his death, when he made his final appearance, which was at the Teatro dal Verme in Milan – venue for the premiere of Puccini's first opera *Le Villi*.

POLONINI, Alessandro (1844–1920)
Bass-baritone who created two roles in *La Bohème* – Benoit the landlord and Alcindoro, Musetta's elderly admirer – and also that of

Geronte in *Manon Lescaut*. Sang in many centres in Italy and also in Spain and South America. As well as Italian roles, he once appeared in Wagner's *Die Meistersinger von Nürnberg*.

POMÉ, Alessandro (1853–1934)
Conductor at the premiere of *Manon Lescaut* at the Teatro Regio, Turin – a theatre with which he had a long association.

PRAGA, Marco (1862–1929)
Playwright, novelist and critic who was approached by Puccini to write the libretto of *Manon Lescaut* and suggested the poet Oliva as collaborator. Left Oliva to complete the libretto when he became exasperated by Puccini's continual changes of mind. Some years later he gave Puccini some help with another project but never collaborated with him again.

RAISA, Rosa (1893–1963)
The first Turandot, and one of the great dramatic sopranos of her time. At the premiere of *Turandot* in 1926 her husband, the baritone Giacomo Rimini, created the role of Ping, and they once appeared together in *Tosca* at Covent Garden, with Rimini as Scarpia. Born Rose Burchstein, she left her native Poland when she was fourteen to escape the pogroms. At her concert debut in Rome in 1912 she greatly impressed the conductor Campanini and he became a guiding light in her career. He took her to Chicago, where she sang regularly between 1916 and 1936. She died in Los Angeles.

RICORDI, Giulo (1840–1912)
Influential Milan publisher who was one of the first to recognise Puccini's potential and refused to abandon him when his business colleagues urged him to do so after the failure of *Edgar*. He paid the composer a monthly allowance to tide him over the difficult period, and guaranteed to repay the firm if the investment failed to pay off. He was instrumental in bringing together the highly

successful team of Puccini, Giacosa and Illica, and as an experienced man of the theatre, his comments on their work were invaluable. He published all the Puccini operas which were completed during his lifetime.

RICORDI, Tito (1865–1935)

Son of Giulio, born in 1865, and took over from him at his death. His relationship with Puccini was not as cordial as his father's had been and it was because he rejected *La Rondine* as 'bad Lehàr' that it was published by Lorenzo Sonzogno. Because of Tito's somewhat autocratic manner, Puccini often referred to him as 'Savoia', which was the name of the Italian royal family at that time. A producer as well as a publisher, the younger Ricordi produced the premieres of *Tosca* and *Madama Butterfly*.

RIMINI, Giuseppe (1882–1952)

Baritone who sang Ping at the premiere of *Turandot*, with his wife Rosa Raisa in the title role. Played the role of Gianni Schicchi with great success.

SCHIPA, Tito (1888–1965)

Tenor who created the role of Ruggero in *La Rondine*. Born at Lecce, he made his debut in *La Traviata* at Vercelli in 1910. He first appeared at La Scala in 1915, when he was successful in *Prince Igor* and Massenet's *Manon*. He was popular in the USA, where he was associated with the Chicago Opera from 1919 to 1932 and with the Metropolitan, New York, from 1933 to 1935. His career continued for some years afterwards, as he was still making appearances in Italy in the early 1950s and toured Russia in 1957, but he never sang in London. He died in Los Angeles.

SIMONI, Renato (1875–1952)

Librettist, with Adami, for *Turandot*. He was also a critic and playwright and succeeded Giuseppe Giacosa as editor of the review

La Lettura in 1906, which may have brought him to Puccini's notice. He had become editor of the newspaper *Corriere della Sera* in 1903, and remained as its music critic from 1913 until his death.

SONZOGNO, Edoardo (1836–1920)
Publisher who inaugurated the Sonzogno Prize for one-act operas, for which Puccini composed *Le Villi*.

SONZOGNO, Lorenzo
Publisher of *La Rondine* in 1917, after Tito Ricordi had rejected it.

STORCHIO, Rosina (1876–1945)
Soprano, born in Verona, who created the role of Madama Butterfly. Like Puccini, she studied at the Milan Conservatoire and she made her debut at the Teatro dal Verme, where his first opera *Le Villi* had its premiere. On that occasion she sang the part of Micaëla in *Carmen*. She sang in the premiere of Leoncavallo's *La Bohème* and was popular in Spain and the USA, where she often sang Mimi. That part and *Madama Butterfly* were good vehicles for her because, although she lacked the vocal and dramatic powers of Raisa and Destinn, she was a very sensitive performer in both her singing and acting.

TERNINA, Milka (1863–1941)
Famous Croatian soprano born in Zagreb, who was greatly admired by Puccini in the role of Tosca, the part which she sang at the London and New York premieres of the opera. Very versatile, including Wagner roles in her repertoire, she taught singing in Zagreb and in New York, where she died. Among her pupils was the great Yugoslavian soprano Zinka Milanov.

TOSCANINI, Arturo (1867–1957)
World-famous conductor, born in Parma, noted among other things for his remarkable memory for musical scores. His association

with Puccini began when he conducted the premiere of *La Bohème* in 1893 at the Teatro Regio in Turin, where he had recently become the musical director. He also conducted the premieres of *Fanciulla del West* and *Turandot*. When Puccini died, his body was placed in Toscanini's family vault until a mausoleum had been completed at Torre del Largo. It was at Toscanini's suggestion that Fidelia's aria 'Farewell, farewell my sweet love' from *Edgar* was played at the funeral service. An outspoken opponent of Fascism, he spent the Second World War in exile from Italy but his career continued successfully for many years afterwards. He died in New York, just two months before what would have been his ninetieth birthday.

VENTURNINI, Emilio (1878–1952)
Tenor who was a good character actor and successful in a number of Puccini roles, including Pinkerton and Spoletta and also Pang, which he sang at the premiere of *Turandot*.

WALTER, Carlo
Bass who created the role of Timur in *Turandot*. Made his debut at La Scala in 1923 in *Rigoletto*, one of several productions under Toscanini in which he took part.

WILMANT, Trieste (1859–1937)
Unusually named Italian baritone who was the first Marcello in *La Bohème*. Sang Lescaut, brother of Manon, at La Scala in 1894 and in the same year took part in *Götterdämmerung* under Toscanini.

ZAMBONI, Maria (1895–1975)
Soprano who created the part of Liù in *Turandot*, although Puccini wrote the part for Gilda dalla Rizza. Born in Peschiera, she sang at most of the larger Italian opera houses between 1924 and 1931, in leading Verdi and Puccini roles, including Manon Lescaut, which she also sang in Massenet's version.

ZANGARINI, Carlo (1874–1943)

Librettist, with Civinini, for *Fanciulla del West* partly because Tito Ricordi thought that, having had an American mother, he would be ideal for the task. Born in Bologna, he confined his activities mainly to libretti, and co-wrote *Jewels of the Madonna* for Wolf-Ferrari. He died in Bologna, where for the previous seven years he had held the chair of poetic and dramatic literature at the Liceo Musicale.

ZENATELLO, Giovanni (1876–1949)

Tenor who began his singing career as a baritone, and created the role of Pinkerton in *Madama Butterfly*. He studied as a baritone in his native Verona and made his debut in as Silvio in *Pagliacci* in 1898, but sang the tenor role of Canio a year later. He had a varied career, singing for some time at La Scala and making regular appearances in Buenos Aires between 1903 and 1910. He made his Covent Garden debut in 1909, but after appearing with the Manhattan Opera in 1907, spent much of his time in America and eventually died in New York. He often sang Des Grieux in *Manon Lescaut*. He and his wife Maria Gay also directed a school for singing and numbered Lily Pons among their pupils. One of his lasting achievements was to begin opera at the Verona Arena, the Roman amphitheatre where performances are still given, appearing as Ramades in *Aida*. He was the manager of the Arena for several seasons.

Arias

'Donna non vidi mai' (*Manon Lescaut*)

Donna non vidi mai, simile a questa,
A dirle, 'Io t'amo'
A nuova vita l'animia si desta,
'Manon Lescaut mi chiamo!'
Come queste parole profumate,
Mi vagan nello spirto,
E ascose fibre vanno a carezzare,
O susurro gentil deh! Non cessar deh! Non cessare!
O susurro gentil deh! Non cessar deh! Non cessare!
'Manon Lescaut mi chiamo!'
Susurro gentil deh! Non cessar! deh! Non cessar! deh!
Non cessar!

Never did I behold so fair a lady,
To tell her, 'I love you',
My soul woke to a new life,
'Manon Lescaut they call me!'
Those words are like perfume to charm me past recapture,
What throbs of passion in my veins are dancing!
Oh what music does dwell in those tones so entrancing,
Oh what music does dwell in those dear tones,
'Manon Lescaut they call me!'

In those dear tones what music dwells,
In those dear tones what music dwells.

'Che gelida manina' (*La Bohème*)

Che gelida manina,
Se la laschi riscalder
Cercar che giova?
Al buio no si trova.
Ma perfortuna è notte di luna,
E qui la luna L'abbiamo vicina.
Aspetti signorina, le dirò con due parole,
Chi son? Chi son?
E che faccio, come vivo –
Vuole?
Chi son? Chi son?
Son un poeta,
Che cosa faccio? Scribo.
Ecco come vivo?
In povertà mi lieta scialo da gran signore,
Rime ed inni d'amore.
Per sognie per chimere e per castelli in aria.
L'anima ho milionaria,
Talor dal mi forzierre,
Ruban tutti I gioielli,
Due ladri,
Gli occhio belli,
V'enar con voi purva,
Ed I miei sogni usato,
E I bei sogni miei, tosto si dileguar!
Ma il furto mon m'accorda,
Poiché, poiché v'ha preso stanza,
La dolce speranza
Or che mi conoschiete,

Parlate voi, deh!
Palate chi riete?
Vi piaccia.

What a cold little hand,
Let me warm it for you.
What is the use of our search?
We won't find it in the dark.
Luckily, it's a moonlit night,
And the moon is very near,
Wait, signorina, I'll tell you in two words,
Who I am, what I do and how I live.
Do you want me to?
Who am I? I am a poet.
What do I do? I write.
How do I live? I get by.
In my carefree poverty I squander rhymes,
and love songs, like a lord.
In dreams and visions and castles in the air,
I've the soul of a millionaire.
Sometimes two beautiful maiden's eyes,
Steal all the jewels from my fortress.
They came in with you just now,
And my customary dreams,
My beautiful dreams,
Melted into thin air!
But I don't mind the theft, for their place has been taken by hope!
Now that you know all about me, you tell me who you are -
Please tell me.

'Si, mi chiamano Mimi' (*La Bohème*)

Si, mi chiamano Mimì
Ma il mio nome è Lucia

La storia mia è breve.
A tela o a seta
Ricamo in casa e fuori
Son tranquilla e lieta
ed è mio svago
Mi piaccion quelle cose
Che han sì dolce malìa
Che parlano d'amor, di primavera di sogni e di chimere
Quelle cose che han nome poesia
Lei m'intende?
Mi chiamano Mimì – il perché non so,
Sola, mi fo il pranzo da me stessa,
Non vado sempre a messa, ma prego assai il Signore.
Vivo sola, soletta là in una bianca cameretta,
Guardo sui tetti e in cielo,
Ma quando vien lo sgelo il primo sole è mio,
Il primo bacio dell'aprile è mio!
Germoglia in un vaso una rosa.
Foglia a foglia la spio!
Così gentile il profumo d'un fiore!
Ma i fior ch'io faccio,
Ahimè! non hanno odore.
Altro di me non le saprei narrare,
Sono la sua vicina che la vien fuori.
D'ora a importunare.

Yes, they call me Mimi,
But my name is Lucia,
My history is brief,
I embroider in cloth or silk, at home or outside.
I am peaceful and happy
And it is my pastime to make lilies and roses
I like these things that have so sweet smell,
That speak of love, of spring,

That speak of dreams and of visions
These things that have poetic names
Do you understand me?
They call me Mimi – but I don't know why.
Alone, I make lunch for myself the same.
I do not always go to mass but I pray a lot to the Lord.
I live alone in a white little room and look up the roofs and sky,
But when the spring comes the first sun is mine
The first kiss of April is mine!
Rose buds in a vase – leaf and leaf I watch it!
That gentle perfume of a flower!
But the flowers that I make,
Ah me! they don't have scent!
I would not know how to tell you about me,
I am your neighbour who comes unexpectedly
To bother you.

'Recondita armonia' (*Tosca*)

Recondita armonia di bellezze diverse!
È bruna Floria, l'ardente amante mia.
E te, beltade ignota, cinta di chiome bionde,
Tu azzurro hai l'occhio,
Tosca ha l'occhio nero!
L'arte nel suo mistero,
le diverse bellezze insiem confonde ...
Ma nel ritrar costei,
Il mio solo pensiero,
Il mio sol pensier sei tu,
Tosca, sei tu!

What subtle harmony of different beauties!
Floria, my ardent mistress, is dark.
And you, unknown beauty, crowned with blond tresses,

Your eyes are blue,
Tosca has dark eyes!
Art, in its mystery,
Blends the contrasting beauties together ...
But in portraying this woman,
My only thought,
My only thought is of you,
Tosca, it is of you!

'Vissi d'arte, vissi d'amore' (*Tosca*)

Vissi d'arte, vissi d'amore,
Non feci mai male ad anima viva!
Con man furtive,
Quante miserie conobbi aiutai.
Sempre con fè sincera,
La mia preghiera,
Ai santi tabernacoli salì.
Sempre con fè sincera,
Nell'ora del dolore,
Perché, perché, Signore,
Perché me ne rimuneri così?
Diedi gioielli della Madonna al manto,
E diedi il canto agli astri,
Al ciel, che ne ridean più belli.
Nell'ora del dolor,
Perché, perché, Signor,
Ah, perché me ne rimuneri così?

I lived for art, I lived for love,
I never did harm to a living soul!
With a secret hand I relieved as many misfortunes as I knew of.
Ever in true faith my prayer rose to the holy shrines.
Ever in true faith I gave flowers to the altar.

In the hour of grief, why, why, Lord, why do you reward me thus?
I gave jewels for the Madonna's mantle,
And songs for the stars, in heaven,
That shone forth with greater radiance.
In my hour of grief,
Why, why, Lord
Ah, why do you reward me thus?

'Un bel di' (*Madama Butterfly*)

Un bel dì, vedremo
Levarsi un fil di fumo
Sull'estremo confin del mare.
E poi la nave appare.
Poi la nave Bianca
Entra nel porto, romba il suo saluto.
Vedi? È venuto!
Io non gli scendo incontro. Io no.
Che dirà? che dirà? Mi metto là sul ciglio del colle e aspetto,
E aspetto gran tempo
E non mi pesa,
A lunga attesa.
E uscito dalla folla cittadina,
Un uomo, un picciol punto
S'avvia per la collina.
Chi sarà? Chi sarà?
E come sarà giunto,
Chiamerà Butterfly dalla lontana.
Io senza dar risposta
Me ne starò nascosta
Un po' per celia
E un po' per non morire
Al primo incontro; ed egli alquanto in pena
Chiamerà, chiamerà:

'*Piccina mogliettina, olezzo di verbena*'
i nomi che mi dava al suo venire.
Tutto questo avverrà, te lo prometto.
Tienti la tua paura – io con sicura fede l'aspetto.

One fine day, we'll see
A tiny thread of smoke rising,
Over the far horizon on the sea
And then the ship appears
And then the ship is white
It enters into the port, it rumbles its salute.
Do you see it? He is coming!
I don't go down to meet him, not I.
I stay upon the edge of the hill
And I wait a long time
But I do not grow weary of it.
And leaving from the crowded city,
A man, a little speck
Climbing the hill.
Who will it be? Who will it be?
And when he arrives
What will he say? What will he say?
He will call Butterfly from the distance,
I without answering
Stay hidden
A little to tease him,
A little so as to not die at the first meeting.
And then a little troubled, he will call, he will call
'Little one, dear wife, little orange blossom.'
The names he called me at his last coming.
All this will happen, I promise you,
Hold back your fears –
I with unshakeable faith wait for him.

'O mio babbino caro' (*Gianni Schicchi*)

O mio babbino caro,
Mi piace, è bello bello,
Vo'andare in Porta Rossa
A comperar l'anello!
Si, si, ci voglio andare!
E se l'amassi indarno,
Andrei sul Ponte Vecchio
Ma per buttarmi in Arno!
Mi struggo e mi tormento,
O Dio! Vorrei morir!
Babbo, pietà, pietà!
Babbo, pietà, pietà!

Oh my dear father,
My love is so handsome.
I want to go to Porta Rossa
To buy the ring!
Yes, yes, I want to go there!
And if my love were in vain,
I'll go to the Ponte Vecchio
And throw myself in the Arno!
Daddy, I pray, I pray!
Daddy, I pray, I pray!

'Nessun dorma' (*Turandot*)

Nessun dorma! Nessun dorma!
Tu pure, o Principessa,
Nella tua fredda stanza,
Guardi le stelle,
Che tremano d'amore,
E di speranza!

Ma il mio mistero è chiuso in me;
I nome mio nessun saprà!
No, No! Sulla tua bocca lo dirò,
Quando la luce splenderà!'
Ed il mio bacio scioglierà il silenzio
Che ti fa mia!
Dilegua, o notte!
Tramontate morir stelle!
Tramontate, stelle!
All'alba vincerò!
Vincerò! Vincerò!

Nobody sleeps!
Nobody sleeps!
Even you, Princess, in your cold chamber,
Watching the stars,
That throb with love and hope!
But my secret is close within me,
None will know my name!
No, no! I shall tell it only on your lips,
When light will shine
And my kiss will break the silence
That makes you mine,
Let the night depart, let the stars set and die,
At dawn, I shall win!
I shall win!
I shall win!